A Baffling Absence

An Arabella Stewart Historical Mystery-Book 4

D.S. Lang

D.S. Lang

Paperback ISBN 978-1-7368385-9-4

Cover Designer: Karen Phillips

Copy Editor: Alyssa B. Colton

Chapter One

"SOMETHING WRONG, LASS?" MAC MacLendon asked when Arabella Stewart returned to the kitchen after answering the telephone in Ballantyne Inn's lobby.

"I'm afraid so," Bella replied as she sat down at the table. "That was Ida Byington."

The older man's heavy gray brows lowered as a frown blanketed his weathered face. "I hope there be nay ailing her parents."

Bella shook her head. "No, they're both fine. It's nothing to do with her family." She gripped her coffee cup and let its warmth spread through her icy hands. Her best friend's call evoked both excitement and uneasiness. Bella was considering Ida's request, but was that wise? With a new resort season about to begin, should she accept? Since Mac was her business partner, he needed to weigh in on the decision.

"Ida is back at school because classes resume on Wednesday. She described the problem, and the headmistress also came on the line." Bella took a sip of coffee before continuing. "They have a difficult situation because Miss Crabtree, the social studies teacher, hasn't returned from her Easter trip, and no one has heard from her. She planned to be on campus no later than day before yesterday. From what they told me, she's frequently late, but it's unusual for her not to wire. As things stand now, they need someone to take her classes this week."

"They have nay heard from her at all?" Mac's frown deepened.

"No, they haven't. According to Ida, Miss Crabtree has no family, so she usually visits a former classmate during school breaks."

"Has the school contacted this friend?"

Bella released a pent-up breath. "No one was home when the headmistress called. I suppose she'll keep trying. In any case, they need a replacement, but I hate to leave you in the lurch."

"Lass, even if we get mild weather, we won't be busy for a few weeks," he said with a grin, "but are ye sure ye want to take on teaching right now? While opening the inn for the Easter holiday was a wise idea, ye've barely had a moment to yeself lately."

What Mac said was true, but Bella wouldn't complain. Having guests for Easter not only enhanced their resort's coffers, the activity had kept her from focusing on past holidays when she'd had family surrounding her. Although she had returned from her duties with the Army Signal Corps more than a year earlier, Bella still felt the losses of her parents

2

and brother quite keenly. She had no idea of how she would have coped without Mac, who was not only her business partner but also her honorary grandfather. "I enjoyed every moment, and the last of our guests left early yesterday, so I had all afternoon to dawdle around the place."

His gray gaze narrowed on her face. "Half of a Sunday is nay much time off."

"It was enough. Besides, the school only needs a replacement teacher temporarily. I'll be back before you know it."

"Ye plan to stay at the school while ye teach?"

"All the staff lives on the grounds," Bella told him. "Ida's room has two twin beds, so I can bunk with her. But, are you sure you can manage without me to cook? Mrs. Rogers is visiting her sister for the next two weeks, and you'll have five of our employees here for meals. Plus, I hate to be away when Griff Biggins hasn't even officially started work as our new golf pro." Indecision still shadowed her thoughts.

"I can handle the shop until he begins on April first," the old pro assured her. "It's only a few days."

Bella scanned Mac's lined face. While she saw no trace of regret, she wondered if he had really accepted cutting his work hours. For over thirty years, he'd been in the golf shop every day throughout the long season. Would he adjust well to the change? Bella certainly hoped so. Mac deserved to take it easy, but she wanted him to be happy doing it. "You like Griff, don't you? I know we agreed it's wise for you to get help in the shop and with giving lessons, but you've been in charge for a long time. You still will be, of course. Griff will report to you."

"I was nay in charge so long, lass. Ye grandfather and I were full partners. After he was gone, ye father took his place and, of course, Matthew came along as an assistant." Sadness clouded his eyes. "I always planned to step away from a seven-day, twelve-hour work week at some point. For a long time, I thought that, when I did, ye father and brother would be the ones to take over."

Bella laid her hand over one of his broad, wrinkled ones. His sorrow echoed inside her. Not a day passed that she didn't think about her parents, lost to the Spanish flu, and her brother, fallen in France. A lifetime of plans and dreams had perished with them. "I did, too. I know hiring a stranger isn't the same, but I think Griff fits in well."

"Aye. Twill be good having him here, and dinna worry about our meals. I can cook breakfast for the group, and we can have sandwiches for lunch. As for dinner, I'll treat the six of us to meals in town for a few nights. In a month, twill be little time to get away. I'm only sorry that ye will be doing more work."

A genuine smile curved Bella's lips. "I'm not sorry. Ida and I will catch up. We haven't had a good chat since she started at Boxmore Hill last fall. Plus, I've always wanted to teach, so this will be fun."

The older man's gray gaze focused on Bella with solemnity. "I know ye always thought ye brother would take over running Ballantyne while ye taught."

Although the war had dramatically changed her life, as it had done to many others, Bella had adjusted. "That was what I planned, but I love Ballantyne as much as Matt did, and I'm happy to be here full-time."

For a moment, Mac sat in silence. When he spoke again, his deep voice was rough with emotion. "I dinna tell ye often enough, lass, that I'm more than happy to have ye here. I know ye family would be pleased and proud of what ye've done in this past year to get the place going again."

"What we've done." Bella corrected him, but her voice held a warm note. "And I agree. They would be happy with both of us. Last spring, I wasn't sure we would have enough visitors to stay open. But we fared far better than I hoped, and the place was filled with guests for the Christmas and Easter holidays. We already talked about refurbishing the tennis courts and opening them this summer. We should think about making a few more boats available, too." Since the resort was on a wide creek near a river, fishing and boating were popular activities.

"Aye, both be possibilities," he agreed. "If we do that, we'll need to hire more help, but we can discuss that after ye get back. When are ye planning to leave, lass?"

"I should be there this evening, if possible. I took enough social studies courses to be comfortable with the material, but I need to know where the girls are in their work. Also, Mrs. Berkey—the headmistress—wants to speak more with me, and I want to meet the other teachers, too." As Bella spoke, she felt the full impact of what lay ahead and hoped she was up to the task.

"Get along, lass, and get to ye packing," Mac advised her. "I'll take care of the dishes and cleaning up."

Excitement bubbled inside Bella. "Thank you, Mac. I want to run into town for a few items, so I'll do that before I pack. Is there anything you need?"

"Nay, lass. Ye go ahead and prepare for ye adventure."

"I'll call the headmistress and let her know I'm coming." Bella couldn't help but smile again. That was how she saw this opportunity, as an adventure and as a dream come true. While, as she had assured Mac, Bella loved Ballantyne, she was pleased to pursue another passion—teaching.

As Bella left the inn, she encountered Griffith Biggins. "Good morning," she said, stopping beside the man.

"Good morning," he replied, sweeping his flat cap off to reveal his close-clipped hair. "You look like you're in a hurry."

"A bit of a rush," Bella agreed before briefly explaining her temporary job. "I hate to leave when you're just getting settled."

His eyes twinkled as he grinned at her. "The little apartment over the shop was in good shape. I'm very comfortable and almost completely situated since I didn't have many belongings to bring." The golf pro paused for a moment. "I was headed to town myself. I want to pick up shaving soap and a new brush. Mine got lost in the move. I'd be more than happy to give you a ride."

"I could drive," Bella said, almost automatically. Some men objected to women motorists. She sincerely hoped Griff wasn't that narrowminded.

Griff's dark eyebrows rose a fraction. "And I'd ride along?"

Something in his tone and expression bothered Bella. "Why not?" After all, she was an excellent driver and a modern woman. He needed to understand the latter.

His eyes shone with something akin to amusement. "No reason. But I want to stop at the filling station and get my vehicle checked over before we get busy. I thought I'd do it today."

"Then, of course, you should drive," Bella said before following him to his Buick roadster. He had a valid reason, and she'd made her point. Griff opened the passenger door for her, and she slipped inside.

"It's too cool to have the top down," Griff observed as he drove away from Ballantyne and toward Moreley. "Perhaps another time." His wide smile and sparkling eyes added weight to the words.

Warmth touched her cheeks, so Bella looked out the windshield. *Another time* could mean anything or nothing. Griff, tall and trim with cocoa brown hair and ice gray eyes, was a very handsome man. In addition, he had a pleasant, affable manner that was engaging. She'd thought so when they'd first met the previous summer, and he'd proven to be an amiable golf partner on several occasions when he'd come to Ballantyne after their initial meeting. Being alone with him in the close confines of his car was new, though. She cleared her throat. "It must be fun to drive." For a moment, she felt his gaze on her before he moved his attention back to the road.

"Yes, it is," he replied. "When you get back from your teaching assignment, we'll have to see that you get a chance to take the wheel."

His friendliness bordered on flirtation, which made Bella uneasy. Despite being in her mid-twenties, she had never had a serious suitor—not that she thought the golf pro was trying to court her. The previous summer, her friend Ida had joined the two of them for golf a few times, and Griff seemed equally pleasant to her, so perhaps he was simply genial with everyone—an excellent trait for a resort employee. With that thought in mind, Bella maintained a casual attitude. "It would be a pleasant change from the Model T."

"I'm sure it would," Griff replied with a laugh.

The drive to Moreley took less than ten minutes. The small town, a few miles south of Lake Erie, was well-situated as a resort location, which was why her Grandfather Stew and Mac had opened their business nearby over three decades earlier. As Bella glanced down Main Street, she felt relieved and proud. When she'd come home at the end of 1919, fifteen months ago, both town and resort were in decline. Circumstances had improved since then, so many establishments were re-opening, and Ballantyne's revival was a big part of the town's rebound.

After Griff parked the roadster in front of the café, Bella got out. Almost immediately, she saw the familiar figure of Constable Jackson Hastings emerging from the café. A tentative smile touched her lips when he stopped a few feet away. Jax had been her brother's best friend. He'd also been her childhood friend, girlhood crush, and occasional escort—all before he'd gone to war as a member of the Ohio National Guard. She had gone, too, as a Signal Corps operator, something that caused the first breach between them. They'd mended the rift, but not substantially. Now, although they'd regained some of their old camaraderie, they were walking completely different paths, paths that only rarely crossed. Over eight months had passed since they'd worked together on an investigation. At the end of the last one, Jax had once again retreated behind his barriers, and Bella saw him only in passing. Like now.

"Good morning, Bella," he said, removing his constable's cap to reveal his wavy blonde hair. As soon as Jax looked at the golf pro, his lips flattened into a thin line of displeasure. "Biggins."

"Nice to see you again, Hastings," Griff said as he offered his hand.

Bella thought Jax hesitated a moment before accepting the gesture. "Good morning, Jax." She strove to keep her voice and expression pleasant and calm.

Some emotion flickered in the constable's green gaze, but his features were carefully schooled as he focused on her. "What brings you to town on such a damp, cold morning? Do you still have guests?"

"No, most left on Saturday and the rest, yesterday," Bella told him. "Now, we won't be busy at the inn until May."

"Naturally, we're hoping the course gets play soon. I'm eager to get started on the season," Griff added. "You know how that is."

Jax stiffened slightly as his attention moved to the other man. "Being a constable doesn't have a season."

His cool, clipped tone made Bella's heart constrict. Was regret in his voice? Probably not. Jax had turned down her job offer—that of being the golf professional at Ballantyne—some time ago. Since then, nothing he'd said or done hinted at second thoughts, but he was good at cloaking his feelings. If he harbored disappointment, he'd likely keep it to himself.

A speculative gleam entered Biggins' silver eyes. "No, I don't suppose it does," he said before turning to Bella. "I need to go to the drugstore before I stop at the mercantile. I'll see you there soon." He nodded to Jax and headed down the street.

Bella glanced back at Jax, who stood watching her with a troubled expression. Suddenly, a gust of wind ruffled his wavy blonde hair, and a lock fell across his forehead. With one hand, he swept it back, but it refused to stay in place. His hair had been close-clipped ever since he'd left for the army nearly three years earlier. Now, while not overly long, it hadn't been cut recently, which wasn't a bad thing. The longer locks made him look younger. Younger and more like the Jax that she had known most of her life. Bella didn't realize her scrutiny was noticeable until he spoke again.

"I need a haircut." He pushed the strands off his face and put his cap, which had been in his hand as he left the café, back on.

Warmth surged into her cheeks, but she held his gaze. "You look fine," Bella murmured. As some indefinable emotion flickered across his face, Bella realized her comment might be misconstrued and hurriedly changed the topic. "I should be on my way. I need to get some things at the mercantile before I get home and pack."

"Pack," Jax echoed. A frown furrowed his brow. "I thought you'd be busy getting ready for the season. Where are you going?"

"Only as far as Boxmore Hill School for Young Ladies," she replied before outlining the situation with the tardy teacher. "If Miss Crabtree gets back soon, I may not be there long at all."

His frown intensified. "The woman isn't back at school and hasn't contacted the headmistress? Aren't they concerned that she might have fallen victim to foul play?"

The green gaze burned with an intensity that was nothing like the old Jax, the one whose passion had been golf, not police work. After explaining Miss Crabtree's late return was not out of the ordinary, although her failure to contact the school was, Bella went on in what she hoped was a light-hearted tone. "You sound like a constable."

Some of the sternness left his face as his lips quirked into a half-smile. "I am a constable."

Briefly, Bella wanted to ask again if he was satisfied with his job, but that would only introduce a highly sensitive subject, one he didn't like to discuss. "To answer your question, the headmistress is concerned."

His amusement fled. "She hasn't called me."

The comment surprised Bella. "Why would she contact you? Boxmore Hill is in the Boxwood jurisdiction."

Jax shook his head. "The Moreley constable's office and the Boxwood office were merged the first of this month. The other small towns that used to be under Boxwood are now with Mitchell Junction, but the school is in our domain."

Bella felt foolish because she had missed this information. Of course, she didn't attend town council meetings and, evidently, she didn't study the local newspaper, either. "I see." She hesitated to ask about staffing because that information had probably been in the news, too. "I'm sure the headmistress will contact you if she doesn't find out where Miss Crabtree is soon."

"I suppose so. You said she got on the train in Minneapolis?"

Bella had provided the information in her summary, so she confirmed the detail. "She did."

"Do you know if she was getting off in Moreley?" Jax asked.

"No, I don't. Maybe so. But no one mentioned her being picked up, so I assume she drove herself. She could have come here on her own or driven up to Sandusky. From there, she'd have to change trains to go on to Toledo and probably change again."

"If she drove over here, someone from the school could easily see if her vehicle is back. I don't suppose the headmistress mentioned that."

"No, she didn't."

Jax looked pensive. "If she has her own vehicle, she might have driven to Toledo. That would save her changing trains once or twice. I'll check with the stationmaster here. He'll know if a teacher from Boxmore Hill bought a ticket and left her vehicle."

His questions and observations were insightful. "You've thought of a lot of possibilities."

Jax shrugged. "Experience helps. I've gotten more than I figured over the past two years. In any case, the woman could have gotten off between here and Minnesota. It's concerning that she planned to be back two days ago but isn't."

"I agree." After helping Jax with three previous cases, Bella wished they could continue discussing the situation. Miss Crabtree's unexplained absence was troubling and intriguing. Not that they had many details to go on. Perhaps, she'd learn more when she got to the school. "I should be going. Ida is picking me up late this afternoon. That way, Mac will have the Ford."

A moment passed before he replied. "How does Ida like teaching? It's a big change for her."

"She's happy to have a job. Besides, she is familiar with Boxmore since she is an alumna. In fact, Miss Crabtree was one of her teachers."

"I know many of the faculty members attended Boxmore Hill. Did Miss Crabtree?" Jax asked.

"She did. From what Ida told me, Miss Crabtree's parents died shortly after she graduated from college. Since they'd been so generous to the school, she was offered a position immediately, and she's been there for over twenty years." Jax's concern made her wonder more about the disappearance, but she was short on time. Reluctantly, she said, "I should get my shopping done."

He nodded. "Of course. I don't want to delay you. Enjoy your teaching and give Ida my regards."

"I'll do both," she assured him before turning toward the mercantile. Before she took more than a step, his voice stopped her.

"Bella, be careful."

When she pivoted to face him, Bella planned to laugh off the admonition until she saw his somber expression. In the past, Jax had admitted to worrying about her safety, especially after she had been kidnapped last spring. Now, Bella nodded but didn't acknowledge his anxiety. He ran hot-and-cold. She might have appreciated his concern more if he didn't stay away from her most of the time. Bella gathered her defenses. She had survived the Great War without his protection, and she'd be fine at a girls' boarding school. "Thanks. I'll be careful and stay safe." As the words came out, she wondered if the same could be said for Miss Crabtree. After working on several big cases, Bella had become something of an amateur sleuth. All of those had involved deaths, but solving a disappearance would be equally challenging and intriguing—if the woman had actually disappeared and wasn't simply late. Time would tell.

Jax watched Bella go with mixed feelings. The teacher's absence put him on edge. Maybe he was thinking like a lawman. Or maybe he was too concerned with Bella's welfare. No matter which, the late return, without notice, was troubling. The distance between Minneapolis and Boxmore Hill was lengthy, and the woman could be any place along the way. If the headmistress was really apprehensive, she would surely contact him soon.

His concern ebbed as he watched Bella join Biggins in front of the mercantile. Jax couldn't hear what they said, but their warm expressions had his gut clenching. Biggins had flirted with Bella when all three met last summer during an investigation. More troubling, she'd reacted in kind. Jax's emotions had been in such a jumble in the aftermath that he'd lashed out at her when, not for the first time, Bella asked why he refused to consider returning to golf as a career. She understood, better than most people, that being a golf pro was his boyhood dream. Two war wounds had forced him to put that aspiration aside. But his physical debility was only one obstacle. Even worse, much worse, he was to blame for her brother's death. As he studied Bella and Biggins, Jax wondered if he should reveal everything and ask for absolution. Almost immediately, he dismissed the idea. How could she forgive him when he couldn't forgive himself?

Fresh frustration filled Jax. He couldn't deny seeing Bella with Biggins bothered him. Not that he had a right to be bothered. Where Bella was concerned, Jax had no rights at all. Despite that fact, he kept observing the scene as she tipped back her head to look up at Biggins. Her brown hair, the color of rich dark chocolate, fluttered in the light breeze. When the golf pro tucked an unruly lock behind her ear, Jax could watch no longer. He turned toward his office and focused on the day ahead. As he did, the situation with the teacher resurfaced. Where was she? What happened to her? If Bella learned anything new, would she call him?

Jax should simply hope the lady returned soon, safe, and sound—but he couldn't help thinking about working with Bella on another case or reflect on the three that they'd already investigated together. She loved sleuthing. Would she do that without him? Probably so, which only increased his worry.

Chapter Two

L ATER THAT DAY, BELLA was unpacking. Although she had not brought a lot, hanging her school clothes in the tiny closet was essential. According to Ida, Mrs. Berkey expected her teachers to wear neat, pressed, clean, and conservative attire. Bella planned to meet that marker on all counts.

"I am so happy you could take Miss Crabtree's place," Ida said, her hazel gold eyes sparkling with obvious excitement. "It will be fun to bunk together again even if the space is rather small."

Bella looked around. The room was larger than she'd expected. It boasted twin beds, twin dressers, two desks with matching chairs, a nightstand, a rocker, and a bookcase. "It's certainly much larger and more comfortable than our last housing in France."

Ida laughed. "That's not saying much."

An answering chuckle left Bella. "No, it isn't." When they'd served as operators near the front lines, their billets had been Spartan and crowded. But they'd only slept while in their quarters, since there had been very little free time for anything else. "This is much, much better. In fact, it's a lot nicer than our college room. Was it designed for two people?"

Her friend nodded. "Yes, when the school first opened, most teachers shared quarters. That hasn't been true for the past few years. As you might expect, enrollment plummeted during the influenza pandemic. It's up this year, but not back to where it once was."

"That's not surprising. Moreley was very hard-hit by flu, and it's not far from here," Bella observed. She tried, but failed, to keep the sadness from her voice.

Ida patted her shoulder. "You know that better than anyone," she murmured in a soft, sympathetic tone. "How was Easter? Did it help to have guests at the inn, or does it make holidays harder? I've been wondering, but I wasn't sure about asking."

Bella looked at her friend's sympathetic expression. Ida had suffered losses, too. Perhaps not as many as Bella, but she understood grief. "You're like a sister to me. You can ask anything," she assured the other woman. "It has helped. I missed Mom and Dad and Matt, of course, but I kept so busy that I didn't have time to feel sorry for myself." She forced a smile and changed the subject. "Both the Christmas and Easter holidays went very well, well enough that Mac and I talked about refurbishing the tennis courts and getting more boats ready this summer."

"That would be wonderful. Then, Ballantyne will be back to normal," Ida said, "and that will help Moreley, which may bring more students back here."

"You might end up with a roommate on a regular basis if that happens," Bella observed with a chuckle.

Ida shrugged. "We'll have to go a long way for such a major change, but it seems possible. Now, if you're finished unpacking, Mrs. Berkey would like to meet you."

Bella looked into the mirror. "I could put on a fresh outfit."

"For any other occasion, I'd suggest that. But our headmistress likes her teachers to dress plainly, so your beige shirtwaist, brown skirt, and serviceable brown shoes will earn approval from her," Ida assured her friend. "Now, let's head to her office. There's a faculty meeting in an hour, so we should get going."

Bella followed Ida out of the faculty residence hall and across the lawn to the main building. As they walked, she glanced at her surroundings. The campus boasted several red brick structures—the teachers' housing unit, a dormitory for students, the classroom building, and a library. A fifth structure, the chapel, was white clapboard. "The library isn't near the main building?" Bella asked as they passed the sign reading *Crabtree Memorial Library.* An arrow pointed to a brick walkway that disappeared as it entered a copse of trees.

"No, the Crabtrees wanted it to be a retreat of sorts. Miss Lansing, the librarian, and Miss Crabtree have offices there. The other faculty offices are in the school itself."

"Why isn't Miss Crabtree with the other teachers?"

Ida paused and turned to face her friend. "Because she is a Crabtree. The rules do not apply to her." Ida's tone was imperious, but she spoiled the effect by laughing. "Basically, she does whatever she wants, and no one finds fault with any of her behavior, no matter how eccentric it is."

"Do the other teachers resent her?"

"A few do, but only a handful have ever expressed any displeasure. They know better."

"Why? What happens?"

Ida's auburn brows lifted a fraction. "Complainers are fired. That's why my predecessor left. Evidently, she was outspoken about Miss Crabtree not only coming back late from holidays but also about her not being required to attend faculty meetings or supervise student activities on weekends."

The revelations painted the missing teacher in an unfavorable light. "How many others have been fired?"

"According to the campus grapevine, at least four in the past few years. In that time, Miss Crabtree has gotten more demanding and less responsible, from what the younger, newer teachers say. The older ones avoid commenting on her at all unless it's to offer a compliment."

"What was she like when you were a student here?" Bella asked.

Ida shrugged. "She was eccentric, but not irresponsible. I never knew her to be late from a vacation, and I was in at least one of her classes all six years that I was a student."

"How strange that she's changed so much."

"Some teachers think Mrs. Berkey is to blame. She's a lovely lady, but not very experienced as an administrator. She's easily influenced and lets board members and big donors dictate to her. Since Miss Crabtree's family also set up an endowment that funds the school on an annual basis, she is one of the most influential donors."

Confusion filled Bella. "If Miss Crabtree is so wealthy, why does she teach? She wouldn't have to work, would she?"

"No, but I think she enjoys being in the midst of everything. She also enjoys lording her power over the rest of the faculty. And there's the fact that her family is gone and she doesn't have many friends. In fact, she goes to visit the same one in Minneapolis every holiday."

Empathy filled Bella. Her family was gone, too, but she was lucky to have Mac. "I wonder why she didn't want to be headmistress. Wouldn't that put her in an even more powerful position?"

"Yes, but she'd also have a lot more responsibility. She wouldn't be able to get away for entire holidays like Thanksgiving, Christmas, and Easter because some students always stay on campus. Mrs. Berkey only leaves during the summer vacation. Even then, she's usually gone a month, no more," Ida said. "Being the headmistress is a demanding job."

"I'm sure it is," Bella said. "And it sounds like Miss Crabtree has an exceptional situation without it."

"She has a lot more freedom than most of the faculty, but she is a fine teacher. I enjoyed being in her classes. She's knowledgeable, fair, and even fun at times. At least she used to be."

Bella put one finger to her chin as she again considered her new responsibilities. "Really? I hope her students won't be too disappointed when I take over her classes." Worry assailed her. After all, she had no teaching experience. What if she was terrible at it?

"They'll love you," Ida assured her. "Everyone does."

Abruptly, Jax's face entered her mind, and Bella blurted out, "Not everyone." She hurried on before her friend asked about Jax, which Ida did all too often. "We should get moving. I don't want to be late for my first meeting with the headmistress."

Once inside the main building, Ida and Bella wound their way through the corridors and stopped at a door labeled *Headmistress.* Ida opened it, and Bella followed her inside the outer office. An attractive woman in her early forties greeted them.

"Good afternoon, Miss Byington," she said before looking at Bella. "You must be Miss Stewart. Welcome to Boxmore Hill School for Young Ladies. I'm Mrs. Ryerson, the school secretary. If I can be of help, let me know. I'll be more than happy to assist you."

"Thank you. I'm thrilled to be here, even if it is for a brief time," Bella replied.

Mrs. Ryerson pursed her lips as all good humor left her face. "It may not be such a short time."

Bella shifted from one foot to the other. The secretary had seemed quite pleasant, but the sudden change in her demeanor was both obvious and inexplicable. Luckily, Ida filled the breach.

"Mrs. Berkey wanted to speak with Miss Stewart before the faculty meeting."

"Of course," the other woman said. "I'll let her know you're here." With that, she strode to the inner office door and stepped inside.

As Mrs. Ryerson rose, Bella couldn't help but notice the woman's attire. While it fit the criteria of clean, neat, plain, and conservative that Ida had mentioned earlier, the gray suit had gone out of fashion some years ago. Bella realized it had not been of the highest quality even when new. After the door closed behind Mrs. Ryerson, she looked at Ida.

"She sounded like she isn't eager for Miss Crabtree to return," Bella said in a soft voice. She didn't want the secretary or headmistress to overhear.

When Ida replied, her tone was equally subdued. "I'm sure she isn't. Mrs. Ryerson has always been very kind to me, and she is to most of the teachers, but most are also pleasant to her."

"And Miss Crabtree isn't?" Bella asked, her curiosity piqued.

Ida shook her head. "No, not at all. I've heard the two of them were classmates and friends at one time. I'm not sure what changed."

"Mrs. Ryerson was a student here?" Bella couldn't keep the surprise from her voice. Boxmore Hill catered to young women from wealthy families, and the secretary looked far from affluent.

Ida nodded. "According to campus gossip, she was from a family as well-to-do as Miss Crabtree's parents. The story is that Mrs. Ryerson married a man who didn't meet her family's expectations, and she was disowned. He was an artist and taught here, but he was fired. Evidently, her parents saw to that. Anyhow, a few years ago, he got ill and died, which left Mrs. Ryerson in a terrible situation. Since she hadn't attended college, the board couldn't give her a teaching position. However, when the secretary post opened, it was offered to her."

"That was kind."

"Yes, but she's a fine secretary. Unfortunately, Miss Crabtree constantly finds fault with her."

"I wouldn't think a teacher would interact with the secretary all that much," Bella said in confusion.

"Most of us don't, but Miss Crabtree goes out of her way to not only interact with her, but to criticize Mrs. Ryerson publicly. I assume she does that when they're alone, too." Her brow furrowed. "There's some longstanding issue between them."

Any further conversation was cut off by the inner door opening and the subject of their conversation emerging. "Mrs. Berkey will see both of you now."

The friends murmured their thanks and entered the main office. As they did, Bella reminded herself to ask Ida for more details on the Crabtree-Ryerson contretemps later.

A tall, slim woman in her early fifties rose from her seat behind a massive walnut desk. She gestured to the two chairs on the opposite side. "Please sit down, ladies." Her attire—a navy suit and white blouse—matched the dress code for her teachers, and her voice had a deep timbre that resonated with authority. Bella wondered at Ida's description of the headmistress as being lax, at least with Miss Crabtree. Perhaps, the woman was more imposing with junior teachers than with major donors.

"Mrs. Berkey," Ida began as she took a chair, "this is my friend, Arabella Stewart."

Bella and the headmistress exchanged greetings.

"Thank you for your willingness to step into Miss Crabtree's shoes on such short notice and for an indeterminate time," Mrs. Berkey said once Bella was seated.

"I'm happy to help," Bella told the older woman.

The headmistress nodded. "We discussed your general duties over the telephone, but I wanted to meet with you. That way, we can get acquainted, and I can provide more detailed information." Mrs. Berkey glanced at a paper on her desk. "You didn't get your degree since you left school to serve in the Signal Corps and you haven't taught before, but you majored in French and English and minored in social studies. Is that right?"

Bella realized the woman must have taken notes during their telephone conversation. Was she checking to make sure Bella had told the truth, or was she simply breaking the ice? "Yes, ma'am. Ida and I left school in the middle of our junior years. After I spoke with you about the courses, I got out my college textbooks and went through some of them. Of course, I'll need to review Miss Crabtree's plans and her materials before classes start."

Mrs. Berkey's dark gaze rested on Bella. "Good. It will be a big undertaking. The girls return tomorrow, and the new term begins the following day. That doesn't give you much time to prepare, so I am exempting you from the usual pre-term faculty duties. You can use the time to get ready for your students."

"Thank you, ma'am," Bella said, but in the back of her mind, she wondered if this was a major mistake. While the idea of teaching was exciting, she already felt overwhelmed. In addition, she couldn't help but mull over Miss Crabtree's baffling absence. Getting ready for her pupils and obtaining more details about the tardy teacher put plenty on Bella's agenda. The latter was hardly a necessity. Nonetheless, it was an interest. A great interest.

After speaking with the headmistress, Bella and Ida attended the faculty meeting. When that ended, Bella went from feeling overwhelmed to being inundated. Mrs. Berkey covered a long agenda with particulars about academic, social, spiritual, and health issues. Academics included both courses and study groups, which meant each teacher not only taught a minimum of four different classes, all of them also supervised four study groups during the week and two on the weekends. Saturdays and Sundays presented more required supervision of extracurricular activities. Bella was still trying to jot everything down when other faculty and staff members started welcoming her. Keeping track of the names was impossible, so she simply smiled and offered thanks for their hospitality.

One of them was Genevieve Lavigne, a petite brunette in her late thirties and Bella's high school French teacher. "Arabella, I am so pleased that you will be teaching with us, even though it is for a short time."

Some of Bella's tension eased. Mademoiselle Lavigne had been one of her favorite instructors at Moreley High School, and she had been the person most responsible for Bella's interest in French language and culture. "Merci, mademoiselle," she said, using the form that her teacher had required in class.

"I was pleased Ida suggested you substitute for Miss Crabtree. I know you'll do a wonderful job." The teacher spoke with certainty.

"As do I," Ida agreed.

"I appreciate the support," Bella replied. Their re-assurances helped, but anxiety continued to plague her as she thought about facing her classes in less than two days.

A speculative gleam entered the French teacher's gaze. "I heard you and Jackson have worked togeth-er on two more cases since the Schwarz murder. How is he?"

Out of the corner of her eye, Bella saw Ida grin and heat rose in her cheeks. "He's doing well."

"Good. He is such a fine young man. I was happy to see both of you last year." Miss Lavigne's ex-pression grew solemn. "I know Mrs. Berkey hasn't contacted Jackson yet, since she is hoping Miss Crabtree will wire or be back. If she doesn't get information today, I urged her to call him. I suppose he already knows about the disappearance."

"He does," Bella replied, although she didn't re-veal he'd heard about it from her. Admitting she'd spoken with him earlier in the day would only lead to more questions about the two of them. Not that there was a *two of them* in any meaningful way.

"What are his thoughts?" the French teacher asked.

"He finds Miss Crabtree's absence worrisome. There's not much he can do unless Mrs. Berkey contacts him. After all, Miss Crabtree could have a good reason for not sending a wire or being back. Besides, even if something is amiss, she may be far from here, since she spent the holiday in Min-neapolis. She could have gotten off the train some place along the way." Despite that possibility, Bella felt as concerned as Mademoiselle Lavigne.

"That seems unlikely," Ida said. "Even though Miss Crabtree seldom makes it back on time, she always wires the school about being delayed."

Miss Lavigne nodded. "I agree, and I'm not the only one who is worried. As Ida said, it's unlike Miss Crabtree not to notify Mrs. Berkey about being late. I haven't known her as long as many other faculty members since I've only been here for three years, but I feel very uneasy about the situation."

Bella glanced at Ida and back at Miss Lavigne. "Mrs. Berkey doesn't seem especially troubled."

The French teacher gave a slight shrug of her narrow shoulders. "I'm sure she doesn't want to create alarm since enrollment is still down. Not that any of the students are in danger, but parents could see a teacher's tardiness as a disappearance, and they might be concerned for their daughters."

Bella chewed on her lower lip. "I suppose they could."

"I'm sure that's true, and Mrs. Berkey has cautioned all of us not to say or do anything that could be construed as negative," Ida put in. "Any hint of foul play could cause some students to leave Boxmore Hill."

The information, coupled with Jax's concern, initiated a new sense of foreboding in Bella. "What did Mrs. Berkey say when you suggested contacting the police if Miss Crabtree isn't found soon?" She directed the question to Mademoiselle Lavigne.

A quick, light breath escaped the teacher. "She said that might be her only option, so I believe Mrs. Berkey will contact Jackson soon, and he will do his usual good job of finding answers," Miss Lavigne said with a smile. "Now, I have a conference with a student who is back early, but I wanted to welcome you, Arabella. Let me know if I can be of any help."

"Thank you," Bella replied.

After Mademoiselle Lavigne walked away, Ida took Bella's arm. "Let's go back to our room before anyone else wants to chat." When they were out of the building, she continued. "It was nice Miss Lavigne asked about Jax. Is he really doing well?"

Bella should have known Ida would use her former teacher's observations to bring up Jax again. Ida used any excuse to promote him as a suitor for Bella. "I think so, but I rarely see him." They'd crossed paths earlier in the day, which was a rarity.

"Why not? Didn't you invite him for Easter? I know he couldn't come for Thanksgiving or Christmas."

"I don't think it's so much that he couldn't come. After all, Jax could ask Nolen Rogers, his deputy, to work a holiday. But he never does. I've invited him for every holiday since I got home," Bella said, although that wasn't quite true. Angry with him for his highhandedness, she hadn't asked him for the first Christmas. Not that he would have come. He never did. "He doesn't want to spend holidays at Ballantyne. He doesn't want to be at Ballantyne."

Her friend shot her a sidelong glance. "That seems strange to me."

"Not so strange. You know he's said being at the resort brings up a lot of memories, and he wants to put all that behind him," she replied. "He doesn't want to be reminded his golf career is over, and I don't blame him. He can barely play nine holes now.

He's thought about surgery, and that might help a little, but there's no guarantee."

"But it could help," Ida replied, "and that could make a difference."

"According to Jax, the surgeon isn't overly optimistic about a big improvement. But I don't want to talk about Jax right now. I have too much else on my mind."

Ida hesitated before saying, "All right. A break before dinner will do you a world of good."

Bella merely nodded and followed her friend back to the faculty residence hall. With so much information crowding her mind, she took no note of her surroundings. Putting one foot in front of the other was all she could manage.

Tuesday morning, girls began returning to campus. Everyone—staff, faculty and students—was welcoming, which Bella appreciated, but she longed for solitude and silence. Her lovely and secluded suite, on the third floor of the inn at Ballantyne, seemed like a distant memory.

By late afternoon, Bella made her way to the faculty dormitory for a brief rest before dinner. Once in the room, she stretched out on her bed and laid completely still. Exhaustion, physical and mental, pressed on her like lead weights. Ida found Bella in the same position when she returned a half-hour later.

"You look exhausted," her friend commented.

"Everyone is congenial, but I felt like I never stopped doing or talking for the entire day. Plus, there's so much to think about in preparing for my students."

"It won't always be like that," Ida assured her. "People want you to feel at home here, and you'll be fine in the classroom."

"Most have been friendly."

Ida's hazel eyes narrowed. "Did anyone not make you feel welcome?"

Bella shook her head. "No, not that. But some people mentioned the murder cases from last year and wanted details."

Ida exhaled sharply. "I should have told you to expect interest. Most of the teachers read the Moreley newspaper, so they know about all three investigations. Some asked me about Laheene's death because they saw stories about it, and the others, as well. Even though your name wasn't in any of the articles, they know you were involved. Boxwood is closer, so teachers usually go there to shop and such. But most travel by train, which means they're almost all in Moreley at some point in the year. Cecil's death was a big topic of discussion when school started last September."

"I only helped investigate," Bella protested. Jax's shoulder and arm problems made both driving and note-taking difficult, so she'd performed those tasks for him. She'd offered her insights and ideas, too.

"From what you told me, you were instrumental in those cases. Miss Lavigne sometimes talks about the Schwarz murder. Other teachers know you and Jax came here to interview her." Ida kicked off her shoes and leaned back on her bed. "I think people may be more intrigued by your insights now because there's a rumor circulating Mrs. Berkey finally reached Miss Crabtree's friend in Minneapolis. At least, the call to her home connected. The friend was out, but the housekeeper said Miss Crabtree planned to be back by late Friday afternoon since she had an engagement in Boxwood."

Despite her fatigue, Bella sat up and faced her friend. "I didn't hear that, but it rules out a stop along the way."

"It does. One of the other teachers was outside the headmistress's office and overheard Mrs. Berkey on the phone. Mrs. Ryerson wasn't around, but the inner office door was ajar." Ida pursed her lips. "From what this teacher said, Miss Crabtree planned on going right to Boxwood from the train station in Toledo. The housekeeper thought Miss Crabtree was quite eager to avoid missing the train because of her appointment. Late Thursday afternoon, her friend took her to the station in Minneapolis and saw her get on, so there's no doubt that she was headed back here."

"Did the housekeeper know what sort of appointment?"

"Not that I've heard."

For a moment, Bella mulled over the information. "Does Miss Crabtree ever get off the train in Moreley instead of going all the way to Toledo on her own?"

Ida shook her head. "No, from what I heard today, she always drives to Toledo and leaves her car at the station there. That way, she can keep her own schedule. She'd probably auto to Minneapolis if it wasn't so far."

"It should be relatively easy to find out if the car is still at the station," Bella observed. "Do you know if Mrs. Berkey is looking into that?"

"Mrs. Ryerson came back to the office before the phone conversation ended, but the other teacher thought Mrs. Berkey mentioned calling the Toledo police."

"With the information she has, that's the logical place to begin." Fresh anxiety played along her nerve ends. Bella had brushed off Jax's admonition, but now she wondered if—as a constable—he'd developed some sixth sense, leading him to know when something wasn't right. And the situation with Miss Crabtree definitely wasn't right.

"Mrs. Berkey may have news at chapel tomorrow morning. She usually has a few announcements, at the very least," Ida said on a yawn. "Right now, I don't know about you, but I'm ready to eat and go to bed."

"That sounds good," Bella agreed, "but I want to go over tomorrow's lessons after supper and before I settle down for the night." Yet, throughout the meal and, even as she reviewed the textbook material and her lesson plans, Bella kept thinking about Miss Crabtree and wondering where the woman could be.

Chapter Three

I DA WAS RIGHT ABOUT announcements. The next morning at the end of chapel, Mrs. Berkey reported the news about Miss Crabtree getting on the train in Minneapolis late Thursday. In addition, the headmistress revealed that a detective at the Toledo Police Department had checked the train station parking area and called back to say the car wasn't there. The police could find no one who remembered seeing the teacher, although the station master recalled the vehicle being in the lot for several days.

As Mrs. Berkey spoke, murmurs rippled through the chapel. Although word about Miss Crabtree's absence had spread through the students as they returned to campus, most were clearly shocked by additional details, as were many teachers. Ida, her face so ashen that her freckles stood out like spots, turned to Bella. "That doesn't sound good at all," she whispered.

"No, it doesn't," Bella agreed. Her mind whirled with a series of questions, but how would she find answers? Should she even try? Bella had to admit, to herself at least, that she wanted to investigate. A slight smile tugged at her mouth. Last summer, during one of their relaxed interludes, Jax had said she was a combination of both her maternal and paternal grandfathers—the lawman and the golf pro. Maybe he was right. She was certainly drawn to both arenas.

"What's so humorous?" Ida asked her.

Bella broke out of her reverie. "Nothing really. I was just thinking about something Jax said last year." Bella didn't realize her error until smug amusement entered her friend's hazel eyes.

"Thinking about Jax? That's encouraging. It was also interesting that Miss Lavigne asked you about him." Ida grinned.

Heat rose in Bella's face. Ida always returned to talking about Jax. And Bella always steered the conversation away from him. When the headmistress signaled dismissal, Bella rose from her seat, grabbed her books, and followed the group now leaving the chapel. "I need to get to class," she said as she hurried out.

Ida's light laughter trailed Bella, as did her friend's words. "You can run from me, but not from your feelings."

A harrumph left Bella, but she couldn't deny Ida's assertion. No, she couldn't deny that at all.

A BAFFLING ABSENCE

After her morning classes, Bella spent a little time preparing for the afternoon and ended up rushing to the dining hall before lunch service ended. The sounds of girlish chatter and laughter reached Bella long before she entered the room. When the clock, in the tower above the main building, chimed the half-hour, she picked up her pace. She needed a few minutes to eat and a few more to sit. The fatigue she'd felt the previous evening was rapidly turning into exhaustion. As she scurried into the main hall leading to the cafeteria, Bella came to a dead stop. Not ten feet away, Jax stood with Mrs. Berkey.

"Miss Stewart," Mrs. Berkey called out, "I was hoping to see you."

Bella joined the pair. "Good afternoon, Mrs. Berkey." Before she could greet Jax, the older woman spoke again.

"I believe you know Constable Hastings since you're both from Moreley."

"Hello, Miss Stewart." His voice and expression were guarded, but not dismissive.

Evidently, he was going to be casual, not familiar, in front of the headmistress. Following his lead, Bella inclined her head and replied, "Hello, Constable Hastings."

If Mrs. Berkey noted the undertone in their exchange, she gave no sign of it. "The constable is here because he's getting a group together to search for Miss Crabtree."

Bella blinked in surprise. "You're going to search around here?"

"As you know, the Boxmore Hill School for Young Ladies is my jurisdiction now," Jax told Bella.

His wink served as a reminder that she hadn't known until a couple of days ago. Since she was substituting as a social studies teacher, someone who should be familiar with local news, she simply said, "Of course."

At that moment, Mrs. Ryerson interrupted. "Mrs. Berkey, you have a telephone call from a worried parent."

"I'll be right along," the headmistress said, before turning back to Jax and Bella. "I am so sorry, but I'll return as soon as I can." She followed the secretary down the hall and out of sight.

"How is the term going so far, Miss Stewart?"

"Today is my first day of actually teaching," Bella told Jax with a trace of asperity.

"I know, but do you like it?" Both his expression and his tone softened.

His overall demeanor revealed genuine interest, so Bella was candid in her reply. "It's an enormous challenge."

"You're up to it," he assured her. The hint of a smile played across his lips.

Those words touched Bella far more than they probably should have, more than either Ida's or Mademoiselle Lavigne's had, so she smiled and thanked him. "I thought it would be very short-term, but now...well, who knows?"

As he nodded, his expression grew solemn. "I'd like to say I have some idea of what happened to Miss Crabtree, but we only know that she left Minneapolis on Thursday, so she could make an engagement in Boxwood. Her friend had no details, but I called the mayor over there after Mrs. Berkey and I spoke earlier. He asked various shopkeepers and a few other people if they saw Miss Crabtree. He discovered she ate at the diner with a local photographer friend."

Her interest was piqued. "Have you spoken with the photographer?"

Jax glanced away, and a long moment passed before he spoke again. "Unfortunately, he traveled to take photographs at some event in Pennsylvania over the weekend, and he planned to stop at a school on his way back. Evidently, he takes a lot of pictures for yearbooks. He should be home late tonight, so I plan to see him tomorrow. I don't want to wait to search for her, though. Boxwood isn't far from the school, and the fact that she's been missing for four days in this area is disturbing. In speaking with the mayor, I learned about some witnesses possibly overhearing her arguing with the photographer when they left the diner. But she was seen driving away alone. With that in mind, we're focusing the search between here and Boxwood. I have a small group out looking already, but it's a large area, so it may take us some time to find—uh—that is, to get answers."

When Jax stammered, Bella figured he'd been about to say *find her body*, not *get answers*. Her gaze narrowed on him. "You suspect foul play."

Something flickered in his grass green gaze, and he nodded his head. "You're too astute, Bella. I don't know about suspecting foul play; it's more that I fear it. The woman was almost back here Friday evening, and no one has seen her or her car since then. It's baffling."

"And unsettling."

"I agree," Jax replied.

"What time was she in Boxwood?"

"From what we know, she left there around six-thirty."

"So, it was almost dark." Bella turned the idea over in her mind. The drive from Boxwood to Boxmore Hill shouldn't have taken longer than fifteen minutes.

"Yep, which makes it more difficult. If it had been earlier, someone might have seen her on the road. After sunset, it's much harder to identify a particular vehicle. The stretch of road between Boxwood and here is well-traveled during summer and fall by both wagons and automobiles, especially during the harvest. At this time of year, there's not as much traffic and few people would take horse and wagon on a major thoroughfare after dark. Too likely for an accident to occur."

"Could she have gotten into a single vehicle crash? A short leg of the highway from Boxwood to here goes along the Boxmore River."

"That's a place we're searching right now. So far, we've found no trace of her or her vehicle."

"By *we*, do you mean you, Nolen, and the Boxwood deputy?"

Jax shook his head. "The part-time Boxwood deputy will start working with us next week. He took some time off this month."

"Can't he come back and help? It seems like you need him now."

"He's in Cincinnati visiting family. I hate to call him, but I may have to do that."

"So, you have a lot more work, but not much more help," Bella observed. "Only one more part-time deputy and the clerk that was hired last fall."

A grin pulled at one corner of Jax's mouth. "That about sums it up. Our mayor and town council still haven't approved of hiring Nolen on a full-time basis. They may during summer, if we get more visitors again. They'll probably sanction additional hours while we search for Miss Crabtree. Right now, the searchers are mostly volunteers. I called Richard Jenkins since he's helped with other cases, but his mother-in-law said he and Jenny are out-of-town."

"That's too bad." The retired senior constable had helped to solve three previous investigations, and his wife had assisted with two. They were both astute and able, and they were amiable, as well. Bella's gaze searched Jax's face. "If Miss Crabtree's car hasn't been found, is it possible she went someplace else? After all, as everyone says, the woman is eccentric. She rarely makes it back here on time, so it seems funny that she would've been a few days early."

"Mrs. Berkey made a point of saying Miss Crabtree has never failed to contact her about being late. But why is she always tardy? My mother was a teacher, and she wouldn't have taken extra vacation time for any reason."

"From what Ida has said, Miss Crabtree has a lot of leeway that other teachers don't."

"I got that impression from the headmistress." Jax glanced up and down the hall before continuing. "I'm here because I wanted to talk with Mrs. Berkey and see if Miss Crabtree had friends in this area, or if she has any ideas on where the woman might have gone when she left Boxwood."

"Did she?"

"No, none at all," Jax said. "Even worse, she told me that Miss Crabtree wasn't close to any of the teachers, although she and the librarian..." His brow furrowed as if in concentration.

"Miss Lansing," Bella supplied.

"Yes, Miss Lansing. Evidently, the two of them were friendly, so I'm going to speak with her before I return to the search. Mrs. Berkey thought we might catch her at lunch, but she left already. I want to talk with the other teachers, too, but not right now." Jax hesitated for a moment as he looked at a group of teachers leaving the dining hall. "I don't want to keep you from your meal, Bella."

Although she would have liked to ask more questions, Bella needed to eat before afternoon classes began. "I only have about ten minutes until they stop serving."

"Go," he told her. "I'll wait for your headmistress here."

Bella still hesitated. Curiosity was a powerful force, but meal times were set, and she couldn't raid the kitchen later like she did at Ballantyne. Finally, she saw no alternative but to leave him without learning more. "It was good to see you, Jax." Why had she said that? She'd seen him yesterday.

For a moment, he simply looked at her. Finally, he nodded. "Enjoy your meal."

"Thank you," she replied, heading into the dining room.

Once Bella had her food, she joined Ida, who was almost finished with lunch and was the last one left at the teachers' table. "I didn't think you were going to make it."

"I didn't, either," Bella admitted, before taking a bite.

"You had a good reason, though." A lilt was in Ida's voice.

Bella, who was eating, raised her eyebrows in question.

"I saw you chatting with Jax." Ida beamed before glancing at the door. "You should've invited him to have lunch with you."

"Oh, Ida. First, I wish you'd stop trying to pair us off. Second, I don't think inviting a man to lunch is a good idea, if it's even allowed," Bella said with consternation. Although her friend meant well, Bella felt uncomfortable when Ida promoted Jax as a potential suitor. The fact that Mademoiselle Lavigne asked about him was another disturbing factor. Nothing serious existed between the two of them. Not that there had ever been more than the possibility of something, even before the war. Ballantyne was her past, present, and future, but it was his past—a past he wanted to forget.

Ida looked back at her friend. "We aren't allowed to entertain men at school unless there's a special event. But Jax was already here. You didn't invite him."

"He's here on official business."

"Really? What did he tell you?" Her teasing tone disappeared as interest surfaced.

Bella relaxed as the conversation moved from Jax as a potential sweetheart to him as a constable. She outlined their conversation. Finally, she wrapped up with "It's very puzzling."

"It certainly is," Ida agreed. "And worrisome, too. Miss Crabtree mostly keeps to herself. None of the other teachers seem to know anything about her life away from here, although she leaves campus every holiday and during the summer. To visit the same friend, evidently. "

"Jax mentioned Mrs. Berkey telling him Miss Crabtree and Miss Lansing were friendly," Bella said.

Ida looked pensive. "They usually sit together at meals, and they were both here when I was a student, so they've been acquainted for years. Neither of them seems particularly warm, but they could be friends. They chat only a little with the rest of us." She paused for a moment. "Is Jax planning to speak with Miss Lansing?"

"Yes, he is." A half-shrug lifted one of Bella's slender shoulders. "He plans to speak with all the faculty and staff members, but he's rejoining the search this afternoon. I suppose he'll be back later today or tomorrow to begin interviews."

"Interviews will mean a lot of note-taking, and Jax still has trouble with that, doesn't he?"

A BAFFLING ABSENCE

Warmth invaded Bella's face, and she glanced back at her plate to avoid her friend's intense gaze. "Writing for a long period remains a challenge, I imagine."

A low laugh escaped Ida. "You've helped him in the past, and you're right here to help again."

Since Bella was thinking the same thing, she could hardly argue. "I have other duties now," she pointed out, "and I'm sure Mrs. Berkey will have someone to help Jax, if necessary. Probably Mrs. Ryerson since she is the school secretary." That idea sent Bella's spirits plummeting, but she struggled to keep her disappointment from showing. If Ida knew how much Bella wanted to assist with the case, she'd continue to play matchmaker. Convincing her friend that her only interest was solving the mystery would be difficult, so Bella didn't plan to try.

"Certainly, Jax will have a voice in who takes notes for him."

Bella wasn't sure what to say to that, but she was saved from further discourse by a bell ringing to signal the end of lunch. She took one last drink of milk before standing up. "I have to get to class, so I'll see you later." She hurried off but, as she went, her mind whirled with the mystery of Miss Crabtree's disappearance, and with ideas of how she might help solve it.

The afternoon dragged. Bella found focusing on her classes and study group difficult, and her students had the same issue. More than a few times, she had to ask them to concentrate on their work. However, she couldn't blame the girls for wondering and whispering about the search for their teacher. The woman's mysterious disappearance was on everyone's mind.

Miss Crabtree's status was also the principal topic of discussion at the teachers' table during dinner. Bella had managed one bite of her food when one of the younger teachers started to chatter.

"It sounds like Crabby may not be coming back," the blonde said in a slightly amused tone.

"That is highly inappropriate, Miss Dobbs. Her name is Miss Crabtree, and we're all hoping she is found soon." Miss Lansing's shrill voice cut through the air like a knife.

Bella's attention immediately went to the librarian, who was a tall, thin, woman in her mid-forties. Even at the end of a long day, not a strand of Miss Lansing's gunmetal gray hair escaped from her neat braid. Nor was a wrinkle visible in the starched white shirtwaist that peaked out from a navy wool serge suit jacket. Everything about the woman said prim, proper, and prudent. Bella wasn't surprised the woman was chastising the younger teacher. Not that the girl didn't deserve it.

At that juncture, Mrs. Berkey took her place at the head of the table. She looked weary and worn, probably from worry. Once all conversation stopped, she spoke. "I talked with Constable Hastings before I came to dinner. They've found nothing helpful yet, but he's planning to backtrack along her route tomorrow morning and look in other areas nearby. He's hoping to get some leads that way."

Murmurs of speculation moved around the table, but Bella didn't contribute. Instead, her mind whirled with the few known details and with ideas of how to solve the case. If she was free, she'd offer to drive Jax. As things stood, Bella had to hope they'd cross paths the next time he came to the school. But when would that be? Her question was answered when the headmistress spoke again.

"The constable would like to speak with each of you, and the rest of the staff, as well. Time is of the essence in finding Miss Crabtree. With that in mind, he wants to do interviews with the staff tomorrow evening and save the daylight hours for searching. He has a great deal to do and a large area to cover with limited manpower." She paused to again look around the table. "The search will continue tomorrow. Due to that, I'm canceling classes. I hope all of you will join in the effort to find Miss Crabtree. Tomorrow after chapel, I'll also ask the girls to help. We'll organize in groups before we link up with the official search parties at nine-thirty."

Those statements set off another round of chatter among the teachers. Finally, Miss Lansing's voice cut through the noise. "I'm sure everyone will be happy to help, as will our girls. Our primary concern now must be finding our colleague as soon as possible."

There were murmurs of agreement, followed by a nod from the headmistress. "I knew I could count on all of you. Now, let's eat dinner before heading to our rooms. We'll need sustenance and rest for tomorrow's venture."

Casual conversation continued, but Bella contributed little. Partly, she was tired. Mostly, she wished she could get more involved in the investigation. How would she manage that? In the three past cases, Richard Jenkins had played a role in getting Jax to involve Bella. Too bad, the senior constable was away. But she and Ida could do some digging. Feeling better about being able to help, Bella continued her meal while her mind reviewed strategies.

Unlike Bella, Jax was still working but, as the sunlight dimmed, he called out to the men walking across the fields with him. "Let's call it a day. It's almost dark, and you should all get home. If you can help tomorrow morning, come to the constable's office about seven o'clock and we'll let you know where we'll be looking." As the men gathered around him, Jax scanned their faces. Most were veterans, men who had fought with him and Matt Stewart in France. At least they were men now. Some had only been boys when they went to war. Serving in the trenches had forced them to grow up fast. "Thank you for your help. Nolen and I really appreciate it."

A chorus of *you're welcomes*, *sure things*, and *anytime* answered Jax. They were good, reliable, loyal men, and he felt humbled by their willingness to pitch in. As the group headed to their vehicles, his deputy turned to Jax. "It's great of them to help, but a dozen isn't enough to cover all the ground between Boxwood and Boxmore Hill School. Not in a timely manner." Nolen's freckled face was drawn with fatigue while uneasiness clouded his hazel eyes.

Jax released a weary breath. Knowing he could rely on Nolen eased his burden. His deputy was becoming a good lawman, which wasn't surprising. He'd been equally adept as Jax's platoon sergeant during the last weeks of the Great War. "I know. I've talked to the headmistress about having some of the faculty, staff, and students help. She's going to ask them in the morning at their regular chapel. I'll also see about interviewing teachers. It's too late tonight for that, and I don't want to waste daylight hours, but I plan to do it tomorrow evening. That's if we don't find Miss Crabtree before then."

"But you'll need to do the interviews even if we find her, don't you think?"

"It depends on where and how we locate her."

Nolen hesitated before saying more. "You don't think she's still alive, do you?"

Jax let his head drop forward as he massaged his taut neck muscles. "Since we haven't found her car, that seems unlikely, although it's possible she took a side trip. If so, she could be broken down or injured. There are a lot of back roads and empty spaces in the area. With heavy woods in places, it's difficult to see any distance. But after five days, I'm not optimistic about finding her alive. Nights have gotten chilly. If she crashed and got injured, hypothermia would have taken a toll long before now. The same is true if she ran off the road and into the river." Jax shoved both hands into his pockets. "But you're right about interviewing all the faculty and staff even if she's dead, which I hope isn't the case. I need to go to Boxwood, too, and I'll do that tomorrow morning. The photographer who had dinner with her may have a lead. Or someone who overheard him arguing with Miss Crabtree could know something important."

His deputy glanced away and back. "Are you going to ask Bella to take notes for you?"

Although Nolen had posed a question, it sounded more like a suggestion—a valid one. Not only was Bella's ability to take shorthand a great asset, her insights and intelligence had proven crucial in three previous cases. But now that Griff Biggins was working and living at Ballantyne, Jax was less eager than ever to involve her. Last summer, he'd told her to move on with her life, as he was doing. If she moved on with Biggins, Jax didn't plan to get in the way. He couldn't. "No, the school secretary should be able to do that."

Nolen's gaze grew troubled. "A secretary can take notes, but Bella has a knack for detective work."

Jax gritted his teeth against denying an obvious fact. Being completely honest was unwise. Instead, he aimed for part of the truth. "We're headed in different directions, which she may finally understand, since I made it clear to her last summer. She didn't necessarily agree with my perspective, but we haven't seen much of one another since the

Laheene case. At this point, I doubt if Bella wants to work with me again." Jax didn't mention seeing her with Biggins and how friendly she'd been with the new pro.

Surprise blanketed his deputy's face. "Since she invited you for all the holidays, she can't be too upset."

A half-shrug lifted his good shoulder. "I think that was Mac's doing."

Speculation replaced surprise in Nolen's expression. "I don't know what's up with the two of you, and I won't ask, but you've known each other most of your lives. You were Matt's best friend, and you spent a lot of time at Ballantyne before the war. Asking Bella to help us would be a good way to repair whatever's gone wrong."

Nolen's insight was typical of him. Although still young, his deputy was wiser than many folks twice his age. Part of his maturity was hard-won from his time in the trenches of France. Another portion came from shouldering family responsibilities. Since Jax couldn't deny that smoothing over the situation was the grown-up way to proceed, he hesitated. Nolen didn't know Jax had turned down working at Ballantyne a year ago. He didn't know Jax had told Bella that they both needed to put the past behind them and move forward. Not that the two of them had much personal to move past. Before the war, they'd only had the possibility of more than friendship. Maybe a remote possibility.

When Jax remained silent, Nolen continued. "You don't want to be at odds with Bella, do you? I mean—again, it's not my business and you are my boss—but I thought…well, I thought there was something between the two of you."

The observation caught Jax off-guard, and his immediate response was to ask a question instead of responding directly. "Why would you think that?"

A rueful smile touched his former platoon sergeant's lips. "The second time you were wounded, we had to cut your tunic off, so drying blood—and there was a lot—wouldn't make the material stick to your flesh. We'd all seen the two photographs of you with Matt and Bella, but I found a picture of only Bella in your chest pocket. It was too badly damaged to salvage." Nolen glanced away and back. "I thought she must be special to you. After all, a guy doesn't carry around a girl's picture unless she's someone pretty important."

Jax briefly closed his eyes as he thought about that photograph. After waking in the field hospital, he'd looked for his uniform because he wondered about her picture. When the nurse said the tunic was ruined, he'd known Bella's picture must have been destroyed, too. Now, his supposition was confirmed. Looking back at Nolen, he saw only concern in the younger man's eyes. "You never said anything about it before now."

Nolen shrugged. "I thought you might wonder where it was and ask. But you never did. When you got back to the line, I knew you were struggling to stay on your feet long enough to make it to the armistice." He glanced away and back. "And I knew you were upset over Matt's death and losing men. I didn't think mentioning the photo was the best idea.

Since then, there didn't seem to be a good time to bring it up."

Again, Nolen showed sensitivity beyond his years. "You're right. Losing Matt was a terrible blow. Having more men die so close to the armistice took a toll, too." The losses had more than taken a toll; they had nearly destroyed Jax. He had missed Bella's photo and figured shrapnel had torn through it. Since that seemed like a metaphor for what had happened to his life and his dreams, Jax hadn't asked about it, and he'd tried not to think about it—or Bella. He was still trying. "As far as the picture, it was a relic from the past, but I thank you for not talking about it with anyone else." He hoped Nolen hadn't.

"It wasn't my business, so I've said nothing."

Relief filtered through Jax. Knowing Nolen had seen the picture, determined its significance, and not shared his knowledge, touched Jax deeply. It also made him even more aware of his deputy's deep sense of loyalty. "I appreciate your prudence."

"Yep," Nolen replied, but curiosity was in his gaze.

Dependability and discretion deserved to be answered with honesty, or at least as much as Jax could offer. "You're right about Bella and I knowing each other for most of our lives. I don't know that we would have courted after the war, but she has always been special to me." Never had Jax admitted as much to anyone. Mac MacLendon had guessed. Richard Jenkins, too. And Matt had known. Yet, Jax had never voiced his feelings.

When several moments of silence passed, Nolen asked, "And she isn't any more?"

Jax massaged his neck where stress was tightening the muscles, just as regret was clenching his heart. "I wouldn't say that exactly. It's more I can't go back and be the man I was before the war, and Bella doesn't completely understand that. We aren't in the same place now because I've had to move on to something new, and she returned to her old life."

Bewilderment blanketed Nolen's face. "Bella has been working hard to restore Ballantyne. That's not really going back. She and Mac are trying to make a better future for the resort and for the town. My mother says they're making important changes, like hiring Mr. Biggins. That will give Mac a break, but he can help Bella, too. That's moving forward, don't you think?"

Hearing the new golf pro's name made Jax flinch, but he forced himself to make a benign observation, "Biggins seems competent." Mrs. Rogers was currently taking time off, but she served as the resort's cook-housekeeper, so she'd met the new golf pro.

"He hasn't started work yet, but he's been moving into the apartment over the golf shop. My mother says everyone likes him since they all got acquainted late last summer and fall when Mr. Biggins came to play golf with Bella."

Late summer was after Jax revealed all he could offer her was brotherly concern. He licked his suddenly dry lips. "So, your mother likes Biggins." Was he going to be the only one who found the golf pro annoying?

Nolen nodded. "Yep, like I said, they all do." A moment of silence preceded his next remark. "Especially Bella."

The comment only highlighted Jax's own observations, yet his heart twisted into a hard, tight knot. That knot rose into his throat, and he swallowed convulsively over it in order to respond. "When we met Biggins last summer, during the Laheene case, he and Bella hit it off right away, so I'm not surprised." Surprised didn't even come close to how Jax felt.

"Is that part of the reason you don't want to involve her in the investigation?"

"I'm not sure what you mean," Jax said.

"I mean, you think it might upset Mr. Biggins if Bella works closely with you again."

That suggestion immediately raised Jax's ire, but he bit back an angry retort. Biggins had no role in Jax's relationship—such as it was—with Bella. Over twenty years of friendship between them should count for something, and Biggins ought to accept that fact. "There wouldn't be anything wrong with Bella helping again, and Biggins has no right to decide for her." His deputy's lips twitched so slightly that Jax wasn't sure if Nolen was repressing a grin or not. The younger man's next words didn't offer a clue.

"Why not ask her to help? We need the extra assistance. Even if you call Newton back from vacation, and I know you don't want to do that, he wouldn't get here until late tomorrow. Besides, Bella has more experience in homicide investigations than he does. All-in-all, having her on the team would be useful. It always has been."

Because his deputy was right, and because Jax refused to worry about Biggins' opinion, he said,

"You make good points. I'll ask Mrs. Berkey if she can spare Bella when I talk to the staff and when I go to Boxwood for interviews. I'd like to do that first thing in the morning if you can handle the search party."

"Of course," Nolen readily agreed.

"I'll head to the school now and see the head-mistress. You don't need to go back to the office. Get a ride home. I'll call you later with any updates."

Nolen nodded and joined two volunteers already in an automobile. Jax immediately went to his Chummy and headed in the opposite direction. As he got closer to the school, he became increasingly anxious. What if he couldn't convince Mrs. Berkey to let Bella help? After a moment, he laughed at himself. During the past three cases, he had tried to keep her from being involved, so the current paradox wasn't lost on him. Nolen's comments about Biggins proved to be the deciding factor. Jax didn't consider why.

Within minutes, Jax was in the headmistress's office, explaining his plans to the woman. At first, she seemed suspicious, so Jax gave her a brief history of his relationship with the Stewart family and Ballantyne. He also highlighted Bella's knack for investigations and her working with her constable grandfather on his memoir years back. He wrapped up by revealing why he required assistance. "I was wounded twice during the war. In the right shoulder and bicep. A lot of driving is hard due to shifting gears, and my handwriting is barely legible. Bad enough that I have trouble reading it myself." Heat invaded his face as embarrassment overtook him. Jax rarely referred to his injuries, and he tried not to think about them. But the woman clearly needed an explanation.

After a series of questions from Mrs. Berkey, she agreed to his request. "I'm about to go to dinner. Serving time has ended, but they're keeping a plate for me. Most of the teachers stay to chat after the meal. Why don't you come along and talk with Miss Stewart about your plans? If she's still there."

Fresh anxiety spilled through him. Quickly, he searched his mind for a way to get the headmistress to relay the news. Bella would surely be surprised, and he didn't want to answer questions in front of others. Or at all. After a moment, he said, "I have to get back to the office. I let my deputy go home and I need to make sure nothing has come up while we were on the search. Would you mind speaking with Miss Stewart? You've already told me when I should be here."

Her gaze narrowed on him, but she nodded. "All right. We'll see you early tomorrow, constable."

Bella was about to leave the table when Mrs. Berkey stopped her. "Miss Stewart, I'd like to speak with you for a few moments."

Dismay formed a tight knot in Bella's stomach. Had she done something wrong? She'd been on campus for a few days and only taught one. While it was a challenge, Bella didn't think she was a complete failure. "Of course," she murmured in response.

As Ida passed Bella, she sent her friend a reassuring smile. Other teachers looked at her curiously, but most also smiled sympathetically. Finally, only Bella and the headmistress remained. By then, Bella's anxiety had risen to a crescendo.

Mrs. Berkey's expression softened. "You need not look so worried, Miss Stewart. I haven't asked you to stay after dinner to offer an admonishment."

The words made Bella realize her tension was obvious, and she tried to relax. "Yes, ma'am."

"I wanted to speak with you privately because Constable Hastings was just in my office, and he told me how much you've helped him with previous investigations. He said you've driven and taken notes, as well."

Surprise hit Bella like a physical force, and for a moment, no words made it out of her mouth. Finally, she cleared her throat to dispel the lingering disquiet. "Yes, Jax—er—Constable Hastings was wounded in France, and he still has shrapnel in his right shoulder and upper arm. That gives him trouble shifting gears and taking notes." All of that was true. But why had Jax mentioned it now? And to Mrs. Berkey?

"He told me. He also said you have a flair for detective work." The older woman's gaze narrowed on Bella. "You studied with your grandfather who was a police officer and constable."

Bella's mind whirled with how to respond. What exactly had Jax told the headmistress? Since she didn't know, Bella aimed to be factual but not expansive. "Something like that." As the older woman continued to scrutinize her, Bella shifted restlessly in the chair. Study wasn't quite the right word for her work with her Grampa Morton. When she'd been recuperating from scarlet fever, a young Bella had grown restless and bored after the worst passed. Her grandfather, a former detective and retired constable, had entertained her with tales of his cases. The two of them had created a memoir, and Bella had been fascinated enough to imagine following in his footsteps until she'd gotten well and changed her goals.

"The constable said you were invaluable in the other investigations. He sounded as if they wouldn't have been solved without you."

The additional revelations stunned Bella. During the Schwarz and Monticello murder cases, she and Jax had argued when he tried to cut her out. Only the intervention of retired Senior Constable Richard Jenkins had swayed Jax. Even with the Laheene case, Jax had hesitated to involve her. Later, and more than once, he'd admitted she'd been helpful. But why was he singing her praises to Mrs. Berkey? Had he come to the school this evening simply to secure her help? If so, why hadn't he talked to her about it? Bewildered, she said, "I'm sure the constable would have solved the cases without my assistance." The comment was benign and honest. Her role had not been the deciding factor.

Mrs. Berkey looked thoughtful. "You and the constable have been acquainted for many years."

The observation made Bella start in surprise again. His chattiness with the headmistress was unusual because, since the war, Jax had become taciturn with everyone. Since there was no point in denying the truth, she nodded. "I've known him since I was four and he was six. He and my brother Matt were in the same class. Jax often came to Ballantyne when we were growing up."

"The constable said he and your brother were best friends."

"Yes, they were." Bittersweet memories briefly surfaced before Bella pushed them away. She needed to focus on the present.

"It's little wonder that he reaches out to you for help in important investigations," Mrs. Berkey observed.

The headmistress must have come to that conclusion on her own unless Jax had lied. The truth was, he usually tried to keep her away from his cases, and he kept away from her, period, at other times. But Mrs. Berkey didn't need to know he ran hot-and-cold.

Bella wasn't sure what the woman wanted to know, so she made another bland, but honest, remark. "Jax spent a lot of time with my family over the years, so he trusts me." Despite all the changes in him, Bella felt that was true.

"Yes, I thought as much." The older woman paused for a moment. "He asked if I might spare you tomorrow so you can drive him along the route Miss Crabtree would have taken, and he also asked if you could take notes when he interviews people in Boxwood and the staff here. Since I already canceled classes, you'll be free. Of course, whether to help the constable or join the search is completely up to you, Miss Stewart."

Once again, Bella's heart raced with excitement, but she tried to keep that emotion cloaked. "If he needs help, of course. I want to do whatever I can to find Miss Crabtree."

"Very well. I told him chapel ends by a quarter before nine. He'll be here then, so the two of you can talk about his plans for the day."

Although she was still surprised, Bella quickly agreed. "I'll be happy to assist in any way."

After the conversation, Bella returned to her room, still trying to figure out Jax's change of heart. Why was he suddenly seeking her help when, in the past, he'd resisted involving her? That was a puzzle. At least his decision gave her a way to help with the investigation.

Bella was still stewing over the change when she saw a note from Ida. Her friend was tutoring several students and wouldn't be back for another hour. With luck, Bella could be in bed and feigning sleep. If she waited until morning to reveal Jax's request, she wouldn't have to discuss the whys and wherefores of it, only to hear her friend insist Jax saw her as more than a little sister.

Despite losing her betrothed in the war, Ida maintained a romantic outlook, which all too often spilled over into Bella's business, making it difficult to rein in her own fanciful feelings and accept how much Jax had changed.

Chapter Four

THURSDAY MORNING, AS THEY got ready for the day, Bella turned to Ida. "I'm going to Boxwood with Jax to take notes."

"You didn't say anything at dinner," Ida said.

"I didn't know I was going until afterward when Mrs. Berkey asked me to stay behind." After a quick overview of the plans, she said, "Do you know anything about the photographer?"

"Not much. His name is Mr. Hilliard. I've met him because he's come to campus a few times to take photographs. He and Miss Crabtree chat, but not in a way that made me think they were especially friendly."

"Since they argued, maybe they aren't."

"Or maybe they're smitten," Ida suggested with a grin.

"Oh, Ida, you're a hopeless romantic."

"It is possible. In fact, it seems more likely than simply being friends. If that's all they were, why would she hide meeting him for dinner? Now that I think about it, Miss Crabtree has had various excuses to go over to Boxwood alone. I wonder if she was always meeting him."

"How often did she go?" Bella asked.

"Twice a month at least."

"Does she have other friends over that way?"

Ida shook her head. "No, but she has an enemy."

"An enemy. Who falls into that category?" Uneasiness hit Bella. *Enemy* was a strong word, and Ida wasn't prone to overstatement.

"Miss Styles. I took her place after she was fired."

Bella sat down to put on her shoes, but gazed at her friend. "Why would they be enemies?"

"Evidently, the woman complained bitterly about Miss Crabtree's tardiness, highhandedness, and influence on school matters. She and Miss Crabtree argued in front of others, from what I've heard. It continued for quite a while, I guess, and finally Miss Crabtree went over Mrs. Berkey's head to the board of trustees. They immediately terminated Miss Styles." Sadness filled Ida's eyes. "I'm glad to have a job, but Miss Styles was here for almost twenty-five years. At her age, changing had to be hard."

"She's teaching in Boxwood?"

"Unfortunately, no. She's working as a clerk at the dry goods store."

"Oh, my. That's a big change." And not a good one.

"Big and unpleasant, I fear. Mrs. Ryerson eats dinner with her about once a month. She says Miss

Styles is living in a garret above the store." Ida's gaze traveled around her cheerful, cozy room. "The faculty quarters here are so lovely. It must be a terrible come-down."

"I'd think so," Bella said. "I'll suggest we talk with her today. Is there anyone else in Boxwood who was well acquainted with Miss Crabtree?"

"No one I know about." She glanced at the watch pinned to her shirtwaist. "We need to get a move on. We've already missed breakfast, but I don't want to miss chapel and upset Mrs. Berkey even more. Besides, she might have some news."

No news was presented at chapel but, when Bella emerged with Ida, Jax was waiting outside. He immediately moved to meet them.

"Good morning, Jax. It's lovely to see you again, although it's not under the best of circumstances," Ida said.

"Good to see you, too," he replied, "but you're right about the circumstances." His attention went to Bella. "Are you ready? I'd like to get going, so I can join the search party this afternoon."

"I'm all set," she replied.

"Good luck," Ida said. "I'll be helping with the search, but I'll see the two of you later."

Jax nodded. "I'm hoping to wrap up interviews in the Boxwood area by early afternoon and be back here by five o'clock. I can begin interviewing the staff after dinner. Of course, that's only if we don't find Miss Crabtree before then."

"Of course," Ida murmured before moving on.

Briefly, Bella watched her friend's retreating figure before glancing around. Scrutiny from the other teachers and some students made her uncomfortable. "Maybe we should go, too."

His gaze followed hers to where a klatch of faculty stood chatting and observing them. "A great idea." Jax opened the driver's door for Bella before going to the passenger's side and getting into the Chevrolet Chummy.

Although Bella was eager to tell Jax about Miss Styles, she was even more eager to voice the question that had been on her mind since the previous evening. Until the air was cleared, concentrating on the investigation was likely to prove challenging. "Why did you ask Mrs. Berkey to let me help you? You've never asked for my help in the past. Instead, you've used a variety of excuses to bar me—my lack of experience, needing to keep me safe, not wanting reminders of the past, not liking that I badger you about giving up your dream."

A harsh breath left him. "I never said all that."

"It's what you meant. However, to Mrs. Berkey, you made it sound like we're still close friends and that you welcomed my participation in past cases when nothing could be further from the truth." Bella heard the edge in her voice, but she wanted answers. Since late August, she'd seen little of Jax. He'd turned down her invitations to play golf and, even worse, they'd had a heated exchange toward the end of the last investigation. At that point, he'd explicitly told Bella to move on with her life like he was doing. Now, he'd enthusiastically sought her help—or so the headmistress had indicated. What did it mean? Something significant?

An uncomfortable silence filled the close confines of the Chummy before Jax replied. "You make it sound like we're enemies, Bella."

The comment angered her because he needn't overstate matters. "Not enemies, but certainly not dear friends. You've made it clear that you're a different man now. A man who doesn't want to be around Ballantyne or me because both evoke memories you prefer to forget. And you asserted I'm both foolish and childish for cherishing those same memories." Being more circumspect might be wise, since he could change his mind about her being involved in the investigation, but Bella wanted answers.

Jax took a long, low breath. "That's not exactly what I said, although I understand why you might have misinterpreted me. I'm sorry for being dismissive. I was upset when you brought up my golf career. I wish I could be a pro again, but it's impossible." He paused for a moment. "I know we haven't talked at length since the last case, but you aren't childish, and you aren't foolish to honor the past. You aren't weak, either. You're stronger than I am because you're at Ballantyne every day, and it can't be easy to face the empty places left by your parents and Matt."

His assertions resonated in her heart, and Bella blinked hard to keep sudden tears at bay. "It isn't, but I know they'd be glad that Mac and I are fighting to keep Ballantyne."

"I know they would be, too." His voice sounded hoarse, and Jax paused briefly before saying, "I hope you can forgive me for what I said last summer. There's no excuse for it, and I should have apologized long before now. That's on me. I suppose I reacted so strongly out of frustration, although it's not a good reason, and I am truly sorry."

Briefly, she considered his words and tone. Jax sounded sincere, and she believed him, mostly because he had acted completely out of character with his criticism. "Thank you," she murmured, "and I won't mention your golf career again."

Again, he hesitated before responding. "I wish I could resurrect it. I wish for a lot of things, but wishing isn't productive. Wishing doesn't change facts."

For several moments, Bella absorbed his admissions and demeanor. Uncertain what to make of them, she said, "I understand." But she wasn't sure she did. She was sure digging deeper wasn't likely to make matters better.

He cleared his throat. "You haven't said if you forgive me for my stupid remarks."

She had trouble suppressing a grin when she responded. "You haven't said if you'll stop making lame excuses to keep me out of cases when I can help."

His expression softened. "I won't accuse you of living in the past. I won't say you're too inexperienced, either," he promised, his own tone solemn. "As far as worrying about your safety in certain situations, I can't pledge not to do that. You're a good detective, but you aren't an officer of the law, and you aren't armed. If a dangerous situation arises, I'll want you out of it. You wouldn't argue with Matt if he was here and wanted you to be safe, would you? Big brothers want to protect little sisters."

The sibling reference, one Jax had used more than once, did little to mollify Bella. Unsure how to reply, she turned to look into the distance.

When she didn't immediately respond, he continued but on another track. "Do you agree to listen to me? It's not only for your sake, it's for mine and anyone else who is involved."

Briefly, Bella studied his face and noted the genuine concern there. "When you put it that way, I can hardly object."

He grinned. "Good. You might keep in mind that I don't let just anyone drive the Chummy." When she smiled back, he released a pent-up breath.

"Driving the Chummy is still a treat," Bella replied as the knot in her stomach loosened.

"It is a wonderful car."

After a sidelong glance at him, Bella said, "Once you have the surgery, you'll be able to drive yourself every place."

"I'm not sure about going ahead with it."

The comment surprised her. "You said the surgeon was a little optimistic."

Several moments of silence passed before he replied. "We'll see. In any case, I'm grateful you agreed to drive and take notes today. Of course, I'll want your opinion on whatever we learn."

His statement was probably meant to placate her, and it succeeded. Feeling better, Bella gave her complete attention to driving. She hated feeling at odds with Jax. He was a strong connection to her past and, although they shared little now, she still wanted him in her life.

After a few minutes, Jax shared his plan. "I want to stop at the diner first. I wasn't able to reach Mr. Jewell, the owner, by telephone, but the mayor planned to tell him I'm coming, and why. Jewell should have details about the photographer, who ought to be back today. I'll talk with him, too."

"I'd heard about a photography studio in Boxwood, which is surprising since it's so small. Ida said Mr. Hilliard, the owner, has been to school to take pictures."

"The mayor said as much to me. Evidently, Hilliard was raised there. He's been working in other places over the past couple of decades and returned last fall. He inherited the family farm and stayed."

"Interesting," Bella murmured. "I wonder if he and Miss Crabtree got acquainted when he took photographs at the school years ago. Ida said they didn't act like they knew one another well, so she was surprised they met for dinner although she wondered if they met regularly."

"Why did she think that?"

"Evidently, Miss Crabtree drives to Boxwood twice a month, always alone. I suppose she could have shopped and eaten at the diner by herself."

"We'll find out while we're there. As far as knowing the photographer, the mayor said Hilliard took pictures for the Boxmore Hill yearbooks before he left town. Miss Crabtree was a student, so they probably met back then, although it's funny if they acted like mere acquaintances when he's been on campus more recently."

"It is odd, but it makes sense that he took pictures years back, since Boxmore Hill was one of the first schools to publish annuals for students."

"Did Ida say if anyone else might have talked about Miss Crabtree visiting with him when she's in Boxwood?"

Bella shook her head. "No. She was speculating about the two of them possibly meeting. I haven't heard anything from faculty members about Miss Crabtree going to Boxwood or about Mr. Hilliard." She let a moment pass before she continued. "I haven't had a lot of time to chat, but a few people asked me about the last three cases we worked on."

"What did you tell them? Hopefully, not a lot."

"Not much, just that they were all challenging."

"But not as challenging as this one. The head-mistress made it clear that she and the trustees want the disappearance solved soon, and so do I. It's really disturbing that a woman is missing."

"You're barely getting started," Bella pointed out.

"True, but we had bodies in the other cases. Now, we have no idea about where Miss Crabtree went, or why she didn't go straight to Boxmore Hill School from Boxwood."

"The search party might find her."

"I hope they do. Have you learned anything else that could be helpful? Anything about her habits or friends or such?"

"I don't know how useful it is, but Ida said that Miss Crabtree is aloof with the rest of the faculty, except for the librarian. Ida doesn't know if they're close friends, but they both have offices in the library and usually sit together at meals."

"Do all teachers have offices there?" Jax asked.

"No, only Miss Crabtree and only because of her family's endowment to the school." Bella briefly shared what Ida had told her about Crabtree's attitude and some faculty members being fired for criticizing her.

"Do you know if any of the terminated teachers live in this area?"

"Only Miss Styles. I know that because Ida took her place when she was fired late last summer."

"Where is she teaching now?"

Bella frowned. "She isn't. She took a clerk job in the Boxwood dry goods store."

"I hadn't heard that from the mayor, but he may not think it's important. Maybe it isn't, but it's interesting. We need to put that place on our list. Working as a clerk seems like several steps down from being a teacher."

"It does, especially since Miss Styles lives above the store, which can't be nearly as pleasant as the faculty rooms at school."

"I'm sure it isn't. Do you know exactly why she was fired last year?"

"She often had words with Miss Crabtree and frequently criticized her. Miss Styles had been doing it for some time. Right before school started last fall, Miss Crabtree went over Mrs. Berkey's head and contacted the board. They fired Miss Styles immediately. That was too late to find another teaching job, I'm sure."

"So, Miss Styles has reason to dislike Miss Crabtree."

"A lot of reason, I'd say," Bella agreed. "The woman taught at Boxmore Hill for almost twenty-five years. Being forced out after such a long time had to be terrible."

"We may turn up more information on her when we talk to the staff this evening, but hearing straight from her would be useful." Jax pulled out a notepad and pencil while he spoke.

"At least we know Miss Crabtree is somewhere in the area."

"Which is good. Otherwise, there'd need to be a search between here and Toledo. Coordinating that would be a nightmare," Jax said. He flipped through his notepad. "I spoke briefly with Miss Lansing, but she wasn't much help. She claimed she was only slightly acquainted with the friend in Minneapolis, but Mrs. Berkey told me that Lansing, Crabtree, and..." He glanced down at his notes. "And Mrs. Charlotte Verson, who's in Minneapolis now, were all in the same class at Boxmore Hill. So was the school secretary."

Bella's forehead furrowed. "I haven't heard about all four of them being in school together. And it seems odd that Miss Lansing wouldn't know Mrs. Verson well. The classes were never large, so all the students should have been acquainted."

"I agree it's strange, but Miss Lansing was quite adamant about not knowing Mrs. Verson well. She admitted to being close with Miss Crabtree, though." A harsh breath escaped him. "I got the feeling she wasn't completely truthful. I plan to interview her again, and I'd like you to be there. Maybe she'll be more open with you around. Just as importantly, your impression of her answers would be helpful. Possibly, I've gotten the wrong impression of her, and she really knows nothing more. Or concern for her friend is making her confused. Anyhow, having you be at the interviews would be good."

"Miss Lansing seems stiff and formal to me. Most of the teachers were very welcoming, but she barely acknowledges me, so she may not admit anything more even if I am present."

"Maybe not, but your note-taking will be useful and I'm sure some of the other teachers will be more comfortable with you there." He shifted to look at her. "I know it will make a long day for you."

"No longer than for you," she said. Her mind returned to other details provided by Ida. "Another thing of interest is Miss Crabtree frequently finding fault with Mrs. Ryerson."

"So, they weren't friends in school?"

"Ida heard they were at one time, but she doesn't know what happened between them. She said Mrs. Ryerson married the art teacher and was disowned by her parents, who disapproved. They also got her husband fired."

"You and Ida have spent a lot of time discussing this case."

His tone revealed little, so she shot him a quick glance before looking back at the road. "I thought it might be helpful if I spoke with Ida."

"Spoke with her." Jax released a loud laugh. "It sounds more like you interviewed her."

Was he really amused? Uncertain, Bella defended herself. "I suppose you should have done the interview. After all, you're the constable."

"I wasn't being critical or snide. As long as the two of you don't do something dangerous, I'm grateful for the information. And it's very useful information, which I desperately need."

"Other teachers will probably know a lot more."

"We'll see later. Now, we should discuss today's itinerary. Let's go to the diner first. This should be a good time to interview the staff, since the breakfast rush is over. I also want to talk to the photographer and Miss Styles."

"Sounds fine."

By the time Bella parked the Chummy on High Street in Boxwood, she was eager to start the interviews. The town was smaller than Moreley, but it boasted a diner and several stores along with a bank, post office, and filling station. Several cars and three wagons were parked on the street, but no one was outside. "It's been a while since I've been here," Bella said as she got out of the car.

Jax joined her on the sidewalk. "I came over last month, but only because we were getting ready to merge offices." His gaze traveled up-and-down the deserted street. "It's a nice little farming community, but it's never been bustling."

"It doesn't look like there are empty storefronts or houses like in Moreley," Bella observed. "Of course, some businesses plan to reopen this spring as our resort season begins, so town won't seem so barren anymore."

"Everyone is looking forward to that, but you're right about Boxwood. They weren't as hard hit by flu and only a couple of their boys died in the war, so the population is virtually the same as it was before. Very small, but stable."

Puzzled by his comment, Bella turned to face him. "If the population hasn't decreased, why were the constables' offices merged?"

Jax shrugged. "According to our mayor, that's been in the plans for years. Once the constable here retired, the process went forward."

"That makes sense," Bella replied as she glanced at the door of the diner. "It looks like you were right about the diner. It's almost empty now."

When they stepped inside, a waitress called out to them from behind the counter. "Sit down any place. I'll be right with you."

"Thank you," Jax replied as he pointed out a corner booth. "How about there?"

Bella nodded. When they got to the booth, Jax helped her with her coat before sitting down himself. "I haven't had breakfast, so I'm going to eat."

"I didn't eat, either, so breakfast sounds good."

By the time they finished, the diner was empty except for the two of them and the workers. Jax had already introduced himself and Bella to Jake Jewell, who joined them after their meal.

"Thank you for taking time to speak with us, Mr. Jewell," Jax said.

The diner owner, a thin man in his mid-fifties, nodded his bald head. "I'm happy to help if I can. Our mayor said you'd be along to ask about Miss Crabtree and Grover Hilliard. She always stopped here, either leaving on holiday or coming back. That's been true for nearly thirty years. When she was a student, she and her parents dined with us going to and from the school."

"So, you've known her well for almost three decades?" Jax suggested.

The man's already wrinkled brow furrowed to create even more lines above his eyes. "Not well, really. Only as a passing acquaintance. We never spoke about anything other than the weather, or the food, or such."

"She didn't talk about the school, her students, or where she traveled on holiday?" Jax asked, surprise in his voice.

"No. Even when she was alone, she kept to herself. She was polite, but she always had a book with her and read while she ate." Jewell paused for a moment. "Except since Grover Hilliard moved back. The two of them have eaten together whenever she passes through town and on other occasions."

"The mayor said Mr. Hilliard took yearbook photographs for Boxmore Hill. Do you know if that's how he met Miss Crabtree?" Confirming his supposition was a viable way to get additional details.

The man nodded. "It is. Years ago now. The two of them met here a few times back then. They've come a lot more often since Grove returned."

"Did Mr. Hilliard join Miss Crabtree and her parents when they were passing through town?" Jax asked.

"Never. Mr. and Mrs. Crabtree were highfalutin folks. Grove's people were farmers, so he wasn't up to their standards, I'm sure. I don't know details, but I'm guessing that's why he was never with them."

"Were Miss Crabtree and Mr. Hilliard courting?" Bella asked.

Since Jax was wondering the same thing, he listened carefully to the diner owner's response.

"That never went far from what I know. Her ma and pa may have gotten on to the two of them stepping out because Grove and Miss Crabtree didn't come in toward the end of her senior year. He took off a month later. Came home for his ma's burial more than a year past and, lately, for his pa's service. Since then, Grove bought a storefront in town. Still living on the farm, but he may sell the land to a neighbor since he's got no interest in farming. He's a darn talented photographer and gets some studio work. Mostly, he goes to schools and such to take pictures. He was going to some big doings over in Pennsylvania over the weekend and stopping a couple of places on his way back."

"Does he go out of town often?" Jax asked.

"Wouldn't say often, but from time-to-time," the diner owner replied.

"Do you know if he left Friday night or Saturday morning?" Jax made the inquiry since timing was crucial.

Jewell shrugged. "He headed out toward his place when he left here on Friday. He coulda gone after that. Don't know for sure." The man shoved his hands into his pants pockets and rocked back on his heels. "He and Miss Crabtree had words after they ate. Loud ones right outside my door. I couldn't tell what they were saying, but several customers were closer. Mr. and Mrs. Sharley were two of them. He told me Grove was going on about how he was tired of Miss Crabtree's snobby ways and, if she didn't want to be with him other than here in Boxwood, she could go to..." His voice trailed off as color rose in his face. "Sorry, miss. I need to mind my tongue."

Bella smiled, but Jax focused on the man's words. "Had they argued in the past?" he asked.

"Not that I know about," Jewell replied.

"Where can I find the Sharleys?" Jax asked. "I'd like names for the other folks, too."

"Sharley owns the filling station." Jewell pulled a small pad from his back pocket and the pencil from behind his ear. He jotted something down and handed the slip to Jax. "About the same time as they were here, Miss Styles was with Mrs. Ryerson, the secretary from Boxmore Hill. The two of them have dinner together once a month. They finished right before Grove and Miss Crabtree. The secretary left a few minutes earlier than they did. Headed over to the drugstore. She probably didn't hear much, if anything, but I'm guessing Miss Styles did."

After asking the owner a few more questions, Jax drew the interview to a close. "Thank you, sir."

Jewell nodded. "Do you want to speak with my counterman now or my waitress?"

"Either is fine. I'd also like to speak with your cook, if she has time," Jax told the man.

"I'll let her know."

The interviews with employees didn't take long, since they had few facts about Miss Crabtree or her relationship with Hilliard. "Let's head to the dry goods store and see if Miss Styles is working. Now that we've got more than one reason to speak with her, I'm really eager to hear what she has to say," Jax said after paying the bill and ushering Bella outside.

"I am, too. It's interesting she and Mrs. Ryerson meet regularly. I've only talked to the secretary in passing, but she must know more about Miss Styles," Bella said.

"I hope so. We can go by the photography studio and stop at the filling station on our way out of town. I'll interview Mrs. Ryerson this evening."

Since the dry goods shop was only two doors down, they arrived in moments. Bella preceded Jax into the narrow front room. Various products filled the shelves lining three walls while displays of ready-made clothing sat in one front window. In the other were several bolts of fabrics suitable for spring and summer. Tables in the middle held a variety of sewing and knitting supplies. The faint scent of roses wafted through the air.

"Good morning. How can I help you?"

The words broke into Bella's thoughts, and she looked behind the counter to see a tall, rawboned woman of middle years. Spectacles perched on her narrow nose, and she peered through them. Her clothing, a white shirtwaist and navy skirt, were no longer in fashion, but they were neat and clean. So was her gray bun.

Bella moved forward with Jax close behind. "Good morning. Would you be Miss Styles?" she asked.

The lady's grin faltered, but she nodded. "Yes, but I don't believe we've met." As Miss Styles spoke, her gaze focused on Jax. "I saw you last month. You're the constable in Moreley, and here now, too." Her voice was devoid of inflection.

"Yes, ma'am." Jax introduced Bella and himself. "If you have a few moments, we'd like to ask you some questions."

"About what?" the woman shot back. Her pale green eyes, alight with suspicion, narrowed on Jax.

He moved to stand beside Bella. "About a case of mine. Can you take a few minutes away from the counter?"

Miss Styles had no chance to answer because another woman emerged from the back room. Her attention riveted on Jax's badge before moving to his face. "I'm Mrs. Kendall, the proprietor. Is something wrong, constable?"

The shopkeeper was a petite, slim woman with pale blonde hair pulled into a French knot. Her attire was far more up-to-date than Miss Styles' clothing, and the fit indicated it was tailored, not ready-made.

"Not at all," he said. After making introductions and explaining the situation regarding the missing teacher, Jax ended with, "I'd like to speak with Miss Styles to see if she knows any of Miss Crabtree's friends or habits. I'm talking with the faculty and staff, and I know Miss Styles only left last fall."

Mrs. Kendall's severe expression didn't soften. "All right." She turned to her clerk. "Take your lunch now. Be back in thirty minutes."

A frown furrowed Miss Styles' forehead as she replied. "Of course." She turned to Bella and Jax. "Follow me. I'll have to eat while we talk."

With that, she disappeared into the back room. When Jax's fingertips touched Bella's back, she followed the other woman, who led them up a narrow, steep stairway. The risers creaked noisily with every footfall. Once they reached the top, Miss Styles turned right and went to a door at the far end of a musty passage. She stepped inside and held the door open.

Bella preceded Jax into a small, cramped room. A dormer window, streaked with dirt, let in a shaft of spring sunlight, but the opposite side of the room lay in shadows. A narrow bed, a battered dresser, and a wooden crate that served as a nightstand filled one wall. Farther back, a table and two chairs sat in front of a cabinet and dry sink. Open shelves held a few plates, a couple of bowls, two mugs, and four mismatched glasses. On the pot-bellied stove, nestling next to the window, were a tea kettle and skillet. A wooden rocker sat beside it. With all four walls bare of paint, the overall atmosphere was one of austerity. As Bella thought about Ida's cheerful room, she felt even sorrier for Miss Styles. What a terrible comedown for her.

"I can fix tea," the older woman said, "but I only have bread and cheese for lunch. No time to cook." As she spoke, Miss Styles prepared her meal.

Evidently, the kettle and skillet were her only cookware. Bella's heart constricted. Once again, she was aware of how fortunate she was.

"Thank you, ma'am, but we had breakfast a short time ago," Jax said. "That's one reason I wanted to speak with you. Mr. Jewell mentioned you were one of those who overheard Miss Crabtree and Mr. Hilliard arguing outside his diner last Friday."

The woman threw a glance over her shoulder before completing her meal preparations and settling in the rocker. "Sit down," she said.

Bella and Jax perched on the rickety chairs at the table. After pulling out a notepad and pencil, she waited for the woman to say more. But it was Jax who broke the silence.

"What did you hear?"

Miss Styles took several bites of cheese before replying. "Arguing."

"What did they say?" Jax asked.

This time, the former teacher ate a chunk of bread before responding. "I don't recall their precise words."

The terse comment made Bella look up. Although Jax's expression remained open and friendly, his gaze had narrowed. If the whole interview went this way, he'd need all of his persuasion to pry information out of the woman. Why wasn't she more cooperative? Did she have something to hide?

"Their precise exchange isn't necessary. A general summary will do," he said.

Miss Styles pursed her lips as if she was sucking a lemon. "Grover said he was done with Miss Crabtree and her snooty ways. He was tired of her only seeing him where folks from the school wouldn't." She took another bite of bread. "That's all I heard. I left right after them. I have Friday afternoons off, and I treat myself to a meal at the diner. Loretta didn't even acknowledge me when they came in or when they left. Of course, she was trying to convince Grover that she wasn't ashamed of being seen with him at the end. Horrible harridan. Always wanting her way and mostly getting it."

"Loretta is Miss Crabtree?" Jax asked.

"Yes," Miss Styles replied. "I don't know why Grover put up with her treating him so shabbily. He deserves a lady who appreciates him for what he is, not someone who was ashamed to be seen with him outside this little town."

The last remark reminded Bella of Mr. Jewell's observations about Hilliard never eating at the diner with the Crabtree family years back. She also noticed that Miss Styles didn't mention the school secretary. Although Jax was conducting the interview, she couldn't withhold an observation. "Mr. Jewell said Mrs. Ryerson ate with you Friday."

The former teacher slanted a sidelong grimace at Bella. "She did."

"He also told us that the two of you meet regularly for dinner," Jax added.

The older woman turned her scowl on him. "Once a month. That's all either of us can afford."

"The two of you must have met at Boxmore Hill School," Jax continued in a smooth, amiable tone.

"We did. Dina is a sweet person, and she was treated shabbily by Loretta, too. Loretta was downright mean with some of us."

Bella noticed the former teacher was referring to Miss Crabtree in the past tense. Was it a happenstance, or was it meaningful?

"We've heard Miss Crabtree and Mr. Hilliard were acquainted when she was a student. Do you know if they courted?" Jax asked.

A harrumph left the older woman. "Her folks wouldn't have allowed such a thing. I've heard tell she introduced them to him at school, but only as the photographer."

"Were you teaching when she was a student?" Jax asked.

The older woman nodded. "She was a senior when I was hired." Tears filled Miss Styles' eyes, and she hastily brushed them away. "I was there for over twenty-five years, and she got me fired because I complained about her highhandedness. Coming back late from every holiday. Having a special office in the library. Being excused from all after-school and weekend activities. Her behavior got worse and worse while she got nastier and nastier with anyone who didn't kowtow to her."

"You being dismissed was very unfair," Bella said, her heart aching for the woman. No wonder she was so taciturn, but harboring hatred was like leaving snake venom inside. Both were poisonous.

"Thank you," Miss Styles said in a tremulous voice. Her gaze surveyed the dingy attic. "I had such a lovely room at school. After so many years, it was my home. I hate to think I'll spend the rest of my life here."

"Have you looked for another teaching job?" Bella inquired.

Miss Styles wiped away the remnants of tears. "I was fired right before classes started last fall, so it was too late. I've contacted several schools in the area and even beyond. Moreley, for one. Perhaps, next year." Her voice grew hoarse, and she took another sip of tea.

"I'm sure you'll find a position by then," Bella said. She certainly hoped so. This barren room was no place for anyone to live.

"Yes, I am, too," Jax added. "I hate to delve further into a difficult topic, but you already know Miss Crabtree is missing. She was here in Boxwood late on Friday. Do you know if she left immediately after arguing with Mr. Hilliard?"

A half-shrug moved the woman's shoulders. "She headed east when she left."

"That's the opposite direction from Boxmore Hill," Bella said.

"Yes, but Grover's farm is in that direction. He drove out before she did. I'm guessing she followed him." The older woman pursed her lips, as if in disapproval.

"Do you think she went there after they argued?" Jax sounded skeptical.

"Possibly," the teacher replied with another shrug.

"Where did you go after leaving the diner?" Jax asked.

The older woman stiffened slightly, and a long moment passed before she responded. "Mrs. Ryerson and I took a drive along the river. That's the only entertainment either of us can afford. The sunset was lovely that evening."

"Do you have a vehicle?" Bella doubted the woman did, but she wondered.

"No. I can't afford one. Dina has an old Packard, so she drove."

"How far did you go?" Jax asked.

"Not far. Gasoline is expensive for folks like us, and Dina wanted to be back at school by eight-thirty. She dropped me off on her way," Miss Styles said.

"Are Mrs. Ryerson and Mr. Hilliard acquainted?" Jax posed another question.

"Of course." Abruptly, the older woman stopped. After a moment, she continued. "He's been taking photographs at the school again. Dina schedules the photographs." Miss Styles finished her meal and sighed. "I need a bit of time to myself before I must return to work."

"Certainly." Jax asked a few more questions before he thanked Miss Styles and followed Bella down the creaky stairs. "Let's chat with the shopkeeper before we move on."

"Sounds like a good idea."

When they emerged from the back room, Mrs. Kendall was behind the counter, and the shop was empty. "May I ask you a few questions, ma'am?" Jax waited until he and Bella were on the other side of the counter before speaking.

Her gaze grew wide. "About the teacher's disappearance? All I know is what I've heard here in town and only since yesterday."

"I understand, but Miss Styles said she had Friday afternoon off, which is why she ate supper at the diner. Did she come back here afterwards?"

Mrs. Kendall seemed to mull over the query. "At some point. I'm not sure when. The last I saw her was when she and the school secretary headed out of town. The two of them get together for dinner once a month. Usually, they take a drive in that old junker of Mrs. Ryerson's afterward. Then, Miss Styles whines for a week about neither of them being able to afford other entertainment. If she thinks I'm giving her a raise, she's wrong."

Jax ignored the shopkeeper's harsh comment. "Do you know which way they headed?"

"East out of town. No idea exactly where." From the way Mrs. Kendall spoke, it seemed she didn't care, either.

He nodded. "Are Miss Styles and Mrs. Ryerson close friends?"

The shopkeeper's expression didn't alter. "I really don't know. Mrs. Ryerson has come to the shop a couple of times. She bought thread and sewing needles. We only exchanged the briefest words. Typically, they meet at the diner, so I don't have social interaction with the secretary."

Jax smoothly moved to another topic. "I understand Miss Styles and Grover Hilliard were acquainted years ago when he did photographs out at

Boxmore Hill, and she was a teacher there. They've renewed the acquaintance since he returned shortly after she moved to town last fall. Do you know anything about their friendship?"

Her lips flattened as if in disapproval. "Miss Styles would like more than a passing connection, but Grover started stepping out with Miss Crabtree shortly after his return."

"What makes you think Miss Styles is interested in Mr. Hilliard?" Jax asked.

Bella wondered herself, so she was glad he'd inquired.

"She always makes a point of chattering away at him if he stops by. Of course, a man needs few dry goods, but Grover bought a couple of ready-made shirts a month ago. Miss Styles ignored other customers to fawn over him." She shook her head as if in disapproval. "If he passes on the street, and we have no shoppers, she grabs the broom and hurries out to clean the sidewalk. So silly for a woman her age to chase after a man, especially one who was clearly smitten with someone else."

Again, Bella felt anxiety tighten her insides. Miss Styles might be too embarrassed to admit interest in the photographer, but how did that influence her view of Miss Crabtree? Since she'd already been critical, could jealousy play a role? To Bella, Miss Styles and Mrs. Ryerson driving east toward the Hilliard farm was cause for concern. Had they followed the teacher? If they had, why?

"So, you have no idea of when Miss Styles returned." Jax sounded as tense as Bella felt.

"No. I was here, in our back room, until around eight-thirty, working on a quilt with some other ladies, and we had a potluck supper along with it. I didn't see Mrs. Ryerson drop her off or hear Miss Styles come in, so her return must have been later."

As noisy as the back stairs were, Bella couldn't imagine Miss Styles slipping silently inside. She cast a sidelong glance at Jax. His voice was well-modulated, but his jaw had tightened. As soon as they left the store, she wanted to go over what they'd heard from the two women and get his perspective. With the additional details, more questions arose. But the same thing had happened in their previous investigations. In the beginning, clues widened the scope. Later, they'd been able to narrow the possibilities. With luck, the latter would happen soon.

"Thank you, ma'am. I appreciate you talking with us," Jax said before escorting Bella outside.

Once they were a few steps away from the front door, she turned to him. "I feel very sorry for Miss Styles, but she has every reason to hate Miss Crabtree, and where was she later on Friday evening? If she and Mrs. Ryerson left town around six o'clock, they only had an hour of light left. Why take a ride in the dark? Especially in an old junker?"

"I'm wondering the same things. What do you think of the school secretary?"

"I haven't gotten to know her very well. I've spoken to her briefly in the dining hall and office. She's always very pleasant," Bella replied.

"She might supply some details when I talk to her. An important one would be when she dropped Miss Styles off and where they went before that."

Bella nodded. "Obviously, Miss Styles lied about when she got home. Mrs. Kendall didn't leave the shop until after eight-thirty, and Miss Styles couldn't have been back by then because she'd walk right by the back room on her way to those squeaky stairs. Mrs. Kendall would have seen or heard her, or both."

"I agree," Jax said. "I want to find out more about Mr. Hilliard and his relationships with Miss Crabtree and Miss Styles. And about Mrs. Ryerson, too. We'll see what he has to say shortly."

Chapter Five

T HE PHOTOGRAPHY SHOP WAS across the street and down a few storefronts. An *OPEN* sign hung in the front window, so Jax opened the door and let Bella go in ahead of him. Within moments, a tall man in his forties emerged from the back. "Good morning, folks. How can I help you?" Jax realized when the man noted his uniform, because Hilliard frowned. "I guess you're not here for pictures."

"No, sir, we aren't." Jax made the introductions and followed with, "I'd like to ask you some questions."

"About Rettie Crabtree?" the man asked. Tension laced his lean frame as he spoke.

"Rettie?" Bella echoed.

"Loretta," Hilliard explained. "I've always called her Rettie."

Jax found the nickname of interest, but didn't re-mark on it. Instead, he said, "Is there a place where we could sit down and talk briefly?"

Several seconds ticked away before a reply came. "Yep. Come in back."

Once again, Jax let Bella precede him. Hilliard gestured to an old sofa next to a potbelly stove and took the rocker across from it. Jax and Bella shared the other seat.

"I won't take too much of your time, Mr. Hilliard, but I'm sure you already know Miss Crabtree is missing," Jax said.

A grim expression blanketed the older man's face. "I heard about it this morning. A terrible thing. I don't suppose you know anything new."

"Not really," Jax replied, "but we're hoping you can help us." Providing information to people wasn't his role as constable. They needed to give it to him.

The man's square jaw tightened. "I don't know how."

"You and Miss Crabtree ate at the diner on Friday evening, didn't you?" Jax kept all doubt and accusa-tion from his voice. Over the past nearly two years, he'd found remaining impassive was the best way to elicit information. Any hint of accusation made people clam up.

Alarm, or perhaps anxiety, clouded Hilliard's hazel eyes. "Yes, but she left right afterwards."

"After you two argued," Jax supplied.

Hilliard's nostrils flared with a sharp intake of breath. "We had a disagreement," he said. "It wasn't the first time. I headed home, and she continued on her way."

"Back to Boxmore Hill?" Jax knew she hadn't, but he wondered what the photographer would say. Miss Styles had said Crabtree followed Hilliard. Would the photographer's story be the same?

"She hadn't planned to go straight there. She was going to have her automobile checked for some issue or another. I'm not mechanical, so I couldn't help her."

"We've been told she headed east, but the filling station is on the south side of town." Jax wondered if the man would lie.

"It is, but she hasn't gone there for service in a couple of years," Hilliard said.

"I thought you'd only been back in town for a few months," Jax said.

"I have, but she told me that last winter. She wouldn't say who was fixing her auto, though." He grimaced. "Trying to make me jealous, I think."

"Was there a reason for her to do that?" Jax asked.

A muscle twitched in the older man's jaw. "None at all, but she liked to toy with people, especially me."

Some emotion shone in Hilliard's eyes. Something akin to hurt. "The two of you have known each other for a long time?" Jax made it both statement and question. After all, more than one person had already said as much, but getting the man's reaction was important.

Hilliard slumped back in the chair. "We met years ago when she was a student, and I did their yearbook photographs. She was a serious, studious girl.

Involved in a lot of school activities. Being year-book editor was one. Back then, few schools published annuals. I was glad to get the job doing their pictures. We worked together a lot and got to be friendly." An almost inaudible sigh escaped him as he looked at the stove. "More than friendly after a while. We were sweet on one another. I was only nineteen. She was seventeen." A wistful note entered his voice and softened his expression.

"You courted," Jax suggested.

The man's gaze met his. "Didn't get to that point. Her folks often came to visit and ate at the diner here. She never invited me to join them, but I met them at the school. All she said was that I did photographs. No hint about us being friends, let alone sweethearts. She was shy, and I figured she didn't want to say how the two of us felt. The next couple of times Mr. and Mrs. Crabtree came, it went about the same. After that, I asked Rettie why she didn't say we were stepping out. Rarely, but I'd picked her up from school and we ate here at the diner or drove to Moreley for a show a few times. She kept it secret from her classmates and teachers. Told them we were going over yearbook pictures." He released a long breath.

"Did she say why she didn't tell anyone about you two being smitten?" Jax asked.

A humorless laugh left the other man. "She didn't want to upset her parents. After all, the two of us were from very different backgrounds, and they expected her to step out with a young man of similar means and education. And not until she attended college. I finished high school, but that's all." His gaze again met Jax's. "My folks were farmers and not wealthy ones, but we weren't poor. I told Rettie I could do well as a photographer, take care of her like she was accustomed, but it would be a while. A few years or so, but I intended to make a mark in the field. It's still a new line of work and few folks are trained in taking and developing pictures. I'd mostly taught myself until I left here. For a time, I worked as a copy boy on a paper in Chicago, and the photographer took me under his wing."

"How did she respond to your plans?" Jax had a good idea, but he needed to hear the details.

"Said her parents would change their minds when I was successful, so we had to wait. Instead of them changing their minds, she changed hers." Hilliard's tone was hard and flat, but emotion burned in his eyes. "At first, she intended to go to college near-by, so we could still see one another. About that time, one of her classmates fell in love with the art teacher. When the girl's parents found out, they got him fired and threatened to disown her if she went ahead and married him. I think Rettie was afraid her folks would do the same to her. At the time, I was in no position to support her, but I didn't think we needed to end everything." He swallowed hard enough that his Adam's apple jumped in his throat. "Right before her commencement, she said we couldn't see each other anymore."

The obvious pain in Hilliard's voice hit Jax hard, and he couldn't help but think of himself and Bella. Was it too late to bridge the widening gap between them? Maybe not. He shifted slightly in order to see her expression, but she was focused on Hilliard.

"What did you say?" Bella asked.

Abruptly, Jax realized his mind had briefly wandered away from the investigation and interview. He couldn't let that happen again but, once Miss Crabtree was found, he'd seriously consider what to do about Bella. Hilliard and Crabtree had wasted over two decades. He didn't want to do the same. But his situation was more complicated.

"I tried to change her mind, but she wouldn't listen. At graduation, she completely ignored me." A shuddering breath left Hilliard. "Even when I took her photograph, she barely spoke."

Jax quickly gathered his thoughts. "And you didn't see her after that?"

Hilliard shook his head. "She came to my mother's funeral a year-and-a-half ago and to my father's last fall. I lived in Chicago for a few years. Started as a copy boy, worked some other low jobs, and finally got to be a photographer. I moved on from there. Only got home from time-to-time. I never contacted her after she brushed me off. She just showed up at the funeral services. After my father's burial, I told her I planned to stay here, and she wanted to get together. I shouldn't have agreed because nothing really changed. She still kept our stepping out secret."

"And that made you mad," Jax suggested.

The other man snorted. "How would you feel, constable, if a lady you cared for kept you at arm's length because you weren't good enough for her?" With one hand, he gestured around the room. The walls were filled with pictures. "I'm a very successful photographer. I not only worked for major newspapers, I did private sittings and made good money. That's why I could afford to buy this place. I don't need to work hard anymore, and after I saw Rettie again, and she wanted to spend time together, I thought we might have a future. But I was a fool."

"Is that why you argued last Friday?" Jax's question was more pointed but, although he felt sorry for the man, he needed to know if rejection and anger had made him lash out.

Hilliard braced his elbows on his knees, folded his hands together, and leaned forward. "I'd wanted her to stay here for the past two holiday vacations. Finally, she agreed to come back early this time, and she did. She still didn't want to court, said we could go on like we were." His hands tightened until his knuckles showed white. "It was more than clear that she never thought I was good enough for her and never would. So, I said what I think. That she's a heartless snob, that she only cares about dictating to others, and lording her money and influence over them. Getting her own way and not caring who she hurts. I said I was done with her."

"How did she react to all that?" Jax asked. The man's words were harsh, but he'd obviously been badly wounded by Loretta Crabtree.

"She tried to deny it, said that wasn't how she felt at all. But actions speak louder than words, and I told her so. Loudly and plainly, I said she was dead to me," he admitted, "but I did nothing to harm her, constable." Both pain and anger were in Hilliard's hazel eyes.

Jax had heard a lot of lies during three murder investigations over the last fifteen months. Whether or not Hilliard was lying remained to be seen. Clearly, his emotions were genuine. "You took off for home, and she headed in the same direction." Jax wondered if Miss Crabtree had followed him to the farm. If she had, would he admit it?

The photographer slumped back in the rocker. "Whoever was working on her auto lives out that way. I don't know exactly where, as I said. She said about fifteen or twenty minutes to the northeast." Briefly, he closed his eyes. When he opened them, they were filled with raw anguish. "But you're right, Rettie followed me to the farm. We argued again, and I told her I didn't want to see her anymore. Not ever. I've got no idea where she went after that. Probably to get the auto checked, as she planned." He paused for a moment. "Come out and look at my place any time, constable. You'll find nothing."

Well aware that he might find nothing even if Miss Crabtree had perished at the farm, and not planning to go with Bella in tow, Jax said, "That won't be necessary today. We're just gathering information. Along those lines, have you known Miss Styles for a long time?"

Surprise flashed across Hilliard's face. "As long as I've known Rettie. Bertha was a young teacher when I started taking photographs at the school. A couple of years older than me. I've seen her a lot more since we're both living in Boxwood."

"Have the two of you ever stepped out?" Jax asked.

A shocked look crossed Hilliard's face. "No, never."

"Mrs. Kendall thinks Miss Styles would be amenable to the idea," Jax said.

A harsh breath left the other man. "Maybe so, but not because I ever gave her reason to think that might happen. She's lonely and struggling. I chat with her when we cross paths. That's all."

When Bella shifted restlessly next to him, Jax glanced her way. She'd stopped writing and her attention was on Hilliard. After he let a pause develop, she spoke.

"You must know Miss Crabtree got Miss Styles fired. What did you think about that?" she asked.

Hilliard rubbed his forehead with one hand. "I didn't know right away. Bertha was at my father's funeral, too. Later, I saw her in the dry goods store. I was surprised about her working there, but I didn't ask why. Soon enough, I found out from others. By then, Rettie and I'd met a few times, so I asked why she did something so unkind. She was full of excuses. I know Bertha can be annoying, and they've had some disagreements in the past."

"Miss Crabtree must have been in some of Miss Styles' classes," Bella said.

"She was, and that was part of the problem. Bertha gave her an *A minus* in literature, which kept Rettie from getting top honors as valedictorian. It upset her terribly at the time and, over the years, her anger built up." He grimaced. "Her parents spoiled her, and Rettie expected to get her way in everything with everyone. It was silly to hold a grudge so long, especially when she got to speak at commencement anyhow."

"Along with the valedictorian?" Jax asked.

The photographer shook his head. "No, that girl wasn't allowed to attend the ceremony. She's the one who fell in love with the art teacher. Dina Ryerson is her name now. The school secretary. After her husband was fired, they stayed in touch, despite her parents' warnings. When they found out, they made her leave campus as soon as her last examination was done. Rettie stayed mad—at Bertha and at Dina. She never spoke about either of them. That's why I had no idea that she'd gotten Bertha dismissed until I heard it in town. I suppose she realized I wouldn't approve."

"I've heard Dina Ryerson and Miss Crabtree were classmates, and that Dina had married the art teacher, much to her parents' disapproval," Bella said. "I suppose it isn't surprising that she and Miss Styles are friendly."

Again, Bella remarked on what Jax was thinking, and he couldn't help but recall his deputy's comments. Bella was far more than a good note-taker and able driver. Her sleuthing skills were top-notch.

"Dina and I were acquaintances back then, and I've only had a few exchanges with her lately, mostly about my work at the school. I don't know any additional details about her marriage to Jeffery Ryerson. I knew him only casually. As a photographer, I take pictures and leave. As far as Dina, she's clearly not rolling in dough, not with that old junker car and her cheap clothes."

"You see her when she and Miss Styles have dinner," Jax said.

"Usually," Hilliard agreed, "but we only speak in passing."

"You said Miss Crabtree and Mrs. Ryerson competed for academic honors. Were they friends?" Jax asked.

"Not when I met the two of them, but they were at one time. Even Rettie admitted to that. She was not only mad because Dina was first in their class, she was very critical about Dina's decision to marry someone so far beneath her." Once again, his features tightened. "I should have realized Rettie would never marry me, but until she said it was over, I was sure she cared more about me than her social status. Even her parents being gone didn't make a difference."

The revelations added specifics, but whether they were meaningful, Jax didn't yet know. When they got back to Boxmore Hill, he intended to find out much more about Dina Ryerson. For now, he had additional questions for the photographer. "Did you discuss Miss Styles' firing when you found out?"

"I told Rettie that she was wrong and ought to apologize to Bertha. She got furious with me, so I let it go. I shouldn't have." Regret lined his face. "I should have stood up for Bertha."

"Did Miss Styles and Mrs. Ryerson come to your farm on Friday evening?" Jax asked.

The photographer's jaw dropped. "No. Why would they?"

Jax shrugged. "They took a drive out your way, so I wondered." Mostly, he wondered if they'd followed

Miss Crabtree to the Hilliard farm. He wasn't sure whether or not to believe the man.

When the bell on the front door tinkled, Hilliard rose to his feet. "I know nothing more about Rettie's disappearance. I have no idea where she planned to go after her auto was checked."

"You don't seem very worried," Bella said.

Jax concurred, so he waited for the photographer's response.

Hilliard stopped and scowled at Bella. "It's not that, but she may have driven back to Toledo to shop once she saw the mechanic. She's done it before. Running off and spending money in town seemed to make her feel more in control when people didn't do her bidding. At least it seemed that way to me. Now, I need to greet my customer. You can use the back door to leave." Any lingering sadness left his voice before he turned on his heel.

As Hilliard got to the door, Jax asked a question of his own. "Are you going to join the search for her?"

The man stiffened, but he didn't turn back. "After this sitting, I plan to look around myself but, like I said, she's probably gone off someplace else." With that, he disappeared into the front of the shop.

Neither Bella nor Jax spoke until they were outside. "Mr. Hilliard had some interesting things to say. He seemed very upset over Miss Crabtree's attitude, but not too worried about her whereabouts for the past few days."

"I agree," Jax said.

"The situation with Mrs. Ryerson, Miss Crabtree, and Miss Styles is certainly food for thought," Bella commented.

"That's an understatement," Jax said with a chuckle. He sobered immediately. "You've learned some helpful bits and pieces from being at the school. Does anything else stand out to you?"

Bella shook her head and fell into step beside Jax as they made their way down the alley and back to the sidewalk in front. "No, but I'll ask Ida if she knows anything that could be useful. Since Mr. Hilliard has taken photos at school recently, I can get her impression of him. He really seemed to care about Miss Crabtree, so it's very hard to understand why he isn't more upset."

"I can't understand it, either. He may honestly believe she went elsewhere for a few days, since he says it's a pattern. Or he wants to believe that. Sometimes, it's hard to accept someone we care about is hurt, or lost, or worse." When she took a sidelong glance at him, Jax cleared his throat. "Of course, his entire attitude could be a front. If she followed him to the farm, and they argued again, he might have killed her. Could have been accidental."

Bella stopped and turned toward him. "Why didn't you want to visit his place today? You might find some clues. Or are you planning to go later when I'm not with you?" When he didn't immediately answer, she continued. "We could go right now. Since he has a sitting, he'll be in town for at least an hour. We could look around outside and see if there are clues to what happened."

Jax shifted from one foot to the other as he mulled over her observation. She was correct about him worrying because Hilliard might follow them. Especially if the man had something to hide. But he would be busy for a while. "You're right. We can go out there now and look around. I doubt we'll find anything since he suggested I go. Let's stop at the filling station for directions and see what the owner heard on Friday since he and his wife are on Jewell's list." When she smiled, he couldn't help but grin back.

Bella and Jax headed to the filling station on the south side of town. Since the drive took only minutes, they didn't discuss Hilliard in more detail.

When she pulled to a stop by the pump, a boy of about seventeen immediately emerged from the garage area. "Morning, need gasoline?" he asked with a grin.

"Yes, fill the tank," Jax said as he emerged from the car. He put his hand out. "I'm Constable Hastings from Moreley, and I wanted to talk with the station owner."

The young attendant shook hands with Jax and said, "I'm Web Sharley. My dad, Chester, is the owner, and he's in the garage. We're working on a car, but go in and tell him you're here."

"Thank you," Jax replied.

As Bella and Jax headed into the car bay, a man came toward them. He was a broader, older version of his son and just as welcoming. A warm smile lit his lined face. "Good morning," he said in greeting. He surveyed Jax's uniform, stuck out his hand,

and introduced himself before saying, "You must be Constable Hastings. I'm on our town council. Sorry I missed the meetin' you were at last month, but glad to meet you."

Jax shook hands with the man and nodded. "Good to meet you, too." He introduced Bella and explained her role. "I need some information, and I thought you might know something to help."

The man's expression grew solemn. "You're looking into Miss Crabtree's disappearance."

Jax nodded. "We are."

Sharley pointed at a battered door with the word *Office* on it. "Please come in and sit down. Happy to help if I can."

The proprietor took a seat behind an old desk while Bella and Jax settled in the two chairs across from him. She pulled out her notepad while Jax began the interview.

"We've heard Miss Crabtree often stopped here to fill up her vehicle," Jax said. He didn't want to provide details. Getting information was his goal.

"Last Friday, she got gas. Miss Crabtree used to have her automobile work done here. In the past couple of years, she's got fuel from us, but nothing done on the car. I asked her about it a few months ago because I was worried about her being unhappy with our service. She said it wasn't that at all, but she had a friend who worked on the vehicle now."

"Did she say who the friend is?" If she hadn't told Hilliard, it was unlikely she'd told Sharley. Still, Jax hoped the man might know more.

"No, only that he lives in this area. Miss Crabtree didn't give no details." Sharley leaned back in his chair. "He'd need knowledge of automobiles, and few have it. That's changing, but I know most who repair vehicles. When I said as much to her, she told me I wouldn't know her friend and changed the subject."

Jax's expectations fell. The man confirmed Hilliard's statement, which did nothing to identify the mechanic friend, so he covered another main point. "Mr. Jewell said you and your wife were outside the diner when Mr. Hilliard and Miss Crabtree argued."

"We was. I always take the missus out for supper on Fridays. As far as what we heard, the gist were Grove got fed up with Miss Crabtree keeping their courtship secret. Don't blame him," Sharley said. "Him and I was in the same class. He finished, and I didn't but I've knowed him all my life. When he started seeing her again, I were worried. She ain't a bad woman, but she's snooty. Might care for Grove in her way, but can't see the two of them ever gettin' hitched, 'specially after last Friday. I think Grove finally figured it out himself."

"What makes you say that?" Jax asked.

"He said he were done with her. She tried to sweet-talk him at first. Then, she got mad too," Sharley replied. "Didn't want no commitment, but didn't want to let him go, neither. Grove stalked off, and she followed. That's all I know."

The man provided more details than Miss Styles, which helped. "I'd like to speak with your wife, too. Is she home?"

"Nope. Visiting her mother up in Toledo for a few days, but she'd say the same as me."

"All right," Jax said. He could interview the woman later, if necessary. "You said Miss Crabtree stopped for fuel. Did the automobile seem to work all right?"

Sharley frowned. "I filled the tank, but it seemed okay and she didn't mention no trouble. Why do you ask? Do you think she broke down somewhere?"

"I don't know," Jax replied. "Mr. Hilliard mentioned she planned to visit her mechanic friend before going back to school."

The man leaned back and looked thoughtful. "She was in a hurry to meet Grove, so I didn't look under the hood."

"I see," Jax murmured. "One other question. Where is the Hilliard farm?"

A line formed between the other man's heavy brows as his frown deepened. "Grove should be in his studio today."

"He is, and we spoke with him. I'd like to drive out that way before we head back to join the search," Jax said.

For several moments, Sharley stared steadily at Jax. "If you're thinkin' Grove had something to do with her not gettin' back to school, you don't know him. He's been sweet on her since they first met. She darn near broke his heart years back. He left town and made somethin' of himself, probably to prove her wrong about him."

Jax noted when Bella stopped writing and glanced her way. She was chewing on her lower lip, as if considering the man's revelations. "Do you have questions, Bella?" She met his gaze, her eyes wide with surprise, but she gave a nod and looked at Sharley. Had he been such a curmudgeon during past cases that his offer took her aback? Jax hoped not. His attempts to keep her out of investigations mostly stemmed from his concern for her.

"Did you and Mr. Hilliard talk about him courting Miss Crabtree?" Bella asked.

A half-smile tugged at one corner of Sharley's mouth. "No, miss, I didn't. None of my business." Solemnity replaced humor. "But Grove wouldn't hurt her. He wouldn't hurt nobody."

"I'd still like to drive out that way, so I'd appreciate directions," Jax put in.

Sharley released a long breath before providing the information.

As Jax got to his feet, a last question surfaced. "Do you know Mrs. Ryerson, the school secretary?"

Again, Sharley got a puzzled look on his face. "She gets fuel here when she's in town, but that's about once a month. We pass the time of day. I give her auto a look-see since it's old. That's about it."

"Thank you, sir," Jax said. "If you think of anything else, please call my office."

The station owner nodded.

After saying their goodbyes, Jax and Bella got back on the road. Almost immediately, she asked, "Do you think there's something important about Miss Crabtree suddenly started taking her car to someone else, someone she never identified to others?"

"Hilliard thought she was trying to make him jealous," Jax said. "I'd say she made up her mechanic friend, but she'd need the automobile serviced in the past couple of years, and she wasn't having it done in Boxwood any longer."

"That's a good point," Bella said, "and it's especially interesting she referred to the mechanic as a friend. From what I've heard at school, Miss Crabtree has very few friends—only Miss Lansing and the woman in Minneapolis fit that category. And Mr. Hilliard, of course."

"Maybe this mechanic, too. Someone else at school might know the person. I'd sure like to speak with him." Jax frowned. "Without a name or a place, trying to locate the guy would be nearly impossible. If we don't come up with any leads today or from the school interviews, I'll get Nolen to check out the garages and dealers in the area, but area is a vague term." Grim resignation resonated in his voice.

"As you said, Hilliard could have lost his temper and hurt her accidentally. There's also Miss Styles. She has plenty of reason to hate Miss Crabtree. She's a sizeable woman, too. Lean but tall. If both she and Mrs. Ryerson held grudges, they may have confronted Miss Crabtree, although it's hard to picture the school secretary doing such a thing. She seems very nice, and everyone likes her."

"Except Miss Crabtree."

"Yes, except for her." Bella paused for a moment. "Do you think Styles and Ryerson might have confronted Crabtree? They were headed in the same direction. Could they have followed her?"

"It's possible, but Hilliard admitted he and Miss Crabtree argued at his farm after first telling us she headed to see the mechanic from the diner."

"Lying is never a good sign," Bella said.

"No, it isn't." He ran one hand over his face. "It isn't necessarily a sign of guilt, though."

"True." Again, Bella hesitated before continuing. "This may be fanciful, but what if the two women trailed Miss Crabtree to the farm and got there after Hilliard inadvertently hurt her? Would they help him cover up?"

Jax tapped his fingers on his knees. "That's three people to keep a secret, which complicates the situation by leaps and bounds. Besides, how well do Mrs. Ryerson and Mr. Hilliard know one another? Well enough for her to get involved in covering up a crime?"

An audible breath escaped Bella. "A good point, but it's possible."

"It is possible, but probable? I'm not sure about that. As far as possibilities, we have a lot at the moment, and I haven't talked to any of the teachers, other than Miss Lansing." Jax mulled over Bella's idea in more detail before presenting additional doubt. "If any of that happened, where is Crabtree's automobile? I keep wondering about it. And, as far as the search, we may be looking in the wrong area. Now that we've talked to people here, she might not be between the town and school, since the mechanic's place is evidently northeast of Boxwood and Boxmore Hill is southeast." The frustration filling Jax crept into his voice. "I should call my office and the school to halt the search until we know more. I hate sending people on a wild goose hunt, especially in this cool, damp weather. What do you think?" He needed another opinion, and Bella was intuitive, intelligent, and insightful.

"I'm not sure, Jax. Why not wait until we check out the farm? That shouldn't take long. If we don't find any useful clues, we could head to the search area, like you planned."

Buoyed by a second opinion, especially hers, Jax nodded. "Let's go out there."

"This must be the place," Bella said as she turned off the road and into a short drive. A two-story frame house sat about twenty feet from the road. Behind it was a large barn. Around the barn were fields, now barren. Farther on was a thick stand of trees. She parked the Chummy by the home, and they got out. The not unpleasant smell of damp earth reached her.

Jax studied the dirt driveway and parking area. "There are a lot of tire tracks."

"Do you think they're from more than two vehicles? I know Miss Crabtree was out here, but can you tell if there was a third automobile?"

He bent down to take a better look. "Not really. All these impressions could have come from two or three cars. Impossible to say. Let's look in the barn. Even if Hilliard harmed her, it's unlikely he'd put the auto in there, but I need to check while we're here."

They stepped into the building, only to find it mostly empty. Some bales of hay were stacked along one wall, but none of the stalls held animals. Nor was there any farm gear.

"It looks like Mr. Hilliard may have sold off the stock and equipment," Bella commented.

"Probably since he may sell the land around the house, like Mr. Jewell suggested," Jax said as he walked the entire interior. "There's no sign of an automobile being in here."

She heard the frustration in his tone. "You didn't think there would be."

"No, I didn't," he agreed, "but I was hoping for solid evidence. Let's look around the woods just to be thorough."

The pair went back outside, headed to the tree line, and followed the path winding through the woods. The farther they walked, the narrower it got until they had to go single file. Jax took the lead. About four-hundred yards from the house, the trees thinned out. Beyond them was a river.

Bella studied the wide expanse. The creek at Ballantyne emptied into the Boxmore River at Moreley and ran through this area before emptying into Lake Erie. "I didn't realize Hilliard's property backed up to water." Bella said when they came to a stop at the river's edge. "Miss Crabtree's vehicle could be in the river. It's deeper and wider closer to the lake."

"It's possible. If Hilliard is guilty, he wouldn't dump it nearby," Jax replied as he scanned the area. "The lake is only a few miles away, and it's a better disposal place. Plenty of isolated places where the car wouldn't be discovered for a long while. Let's look along the bank in the immediate area. She could have lost control and driven off the road, if she passed close to the water. Since we don't know exactly where she headed from here, it's hard to say. I don't want to waste time, but I'd like to walk the bank for a ways. It's pretty muddy, so you could stay here."

Bella pointed to her feet. "I wore old, sturdy shoes. I'll be fine." When he opened his mouth, she felt sure he would object.

Abruptly, Jax nodded. "All right. Let's go."

The pair hiked along the river bank. Only birds chirping broke the silence. After walking for fifteen minutes, they headed backed to where they started.

"This isn't helping much," Jax muttered.

"Part of the road going toward Lake Erie runs along on the opposite side. Not right here, but farther north." Bella pointed across the river. "We could go over there and drive a few miles to see if we find something."

"All right. Another fifteen or twenty minutes won't make much difference. If we don't see anything in that time, we'll head to the search site. Early this morning, another constable drove the section of road going along the river farther to the north. I went over that way on my way to the school and talked to him. No clues there."

"You were up and out early."

"I was hoping the early bird got the worm, but nothing new cropped up."

Chapter Six

THEY HEADED AWAY FROM the Hilliard farm and on to a main road. After going a couple of miles, the river became visible, so Bella continued until it veered away from the highway. Following the route provided no clues.

"Turn around up here," Jax said, indicating a side lane. "Since the water is bending away from the road, there's no sense in going farther. If her vehicle was in the water here, we'd see something. For all we know, her vehicle could be in the lake, some woods, or a barn. And any place in a wide area."

The edge in Jax's voice echoed inside Bella. Helping with three previous homicide investigations hadn't prepared her for a missing person case, but she offered optimism. "We learned a lot in Boxwood."

"A lot of details, but I don't feel any closer to a solution."

He sounded weary, so Bella continued to express positive points. As always, Jax expected too much of himself. "We identified two suspects with Mr. Hilliard and Miss Styles. Maybe a third with the mechanic and, as you said, some teachers might know more about him."

"I hope so, and let's not forget Mrs. Ryerson. I know she seems nice, but that's not a powerful indicator of her behavior, especially with a nemesis like Miss Crabtree." He drummed his fingers on his knees. "Two people working together would have an easier time of hiding Crabtree's car. I'm not saying Miss Styles and Mrs. Ryerson are guilty but, from past cases, we know people can act completely out of character when they hold grudges, especially over a long period."

"Being jilted can create similar powerful feelings," Bella pointed out.

"True. Any of those three could be involved. So could the mechanic, or someone else from school, or a complete stranger."

His summary was valid and disturbing. Finding Miss Crabtree safe and sound and soon seemed less and less likely. "The interviews may prove crucial, and we don't know if the searchers discovered anything."

"We'll be there shortly and find out."

When they got to the search headquarters, which was off the main highway about halfway between Boxwood and Boxmore Hill, Jax directed Bella to the temporary post. Vehicles were parked on the bare ground. As they got closer, Jax saw his deputy with Richard Jenkins. The pair glanced up as Jax and Bella approached them.

"Surprised to see you here, Richard, but glad, too," Jax said, extending his hand to the older man.

Jenkins exchanged greetings with both Jax and Bella. "Jenny and I came home early from our holiday because she caught an awful cold. I was sorry about that, but happy to help you out. Of course, you and Nolen are doing a great job, as always."

"Anything new?" the deputy asked, looking at his boss.

Jax briefly summed up what they had learned about Miss Crabtree, Mr. Hilliard, Miss Styles, and the unknown mechanic. "We're hoping one of the teachers knows more about this friend."

"I hope so, too," Jenkins said, "because it could be a good lead. The situation with Hilliard is of interest. Same with Styles and Ryerson. You uncovered a lot of information. Unfortunately, we've found nothing at all here. We've combed the fields and woods from Boxwood to Boxmore Hill, and we've had groups go back through them at least a quarter-mile. I drove some of the side roads myself. No sign of Miss Crabtree or her vehicle." He ran his short, broad fingers through his clipped gray hair. "This is tough."

"It sure is," Jax agreed, his vexation echoed in his weary tone. "Very tough."

The older man clapped Jax on the back. "Don't let it get to you, son. Looking for a missing person is always difficult because you don't know if it's a planned disappearance, an accident, or a crime. If it's a crime, you don't have a location. At least, in this case, you know the woman was in the general area on Friday evening."

"It's possible she turned back, though," Jax said. "Hilliard said she sometimes goes to the city for shopping when she's upset."

"Possible," Jenkins agreed, "but not too likely, in my opinion. That sounds like a deflection. It was nearly dark when she left Boxwood. Driving to Toledo would take a couple of hours. The stores would be closed. If she has no friends or family there, she'd need a hotel room. But why would she stay there and not wire the headmistress? It doesn't seem like a valid scenario to me."

Jax nodded, glad to have his apprehension minimized. Since Richard didn't swallow Hilliard's story, Jax dismissed the idea, as he didn't find it viable, either. The retired senior constable had years of experience behind him, so his judgment was always useful. "For now, we'll keep searching. Bella has some notes on our interviews, and she'll combine them with whatever you have, Nolen. That way, we'll have everything in one place."

"All right," the young man said as he turned to Bella. "I have my notepad in Richard's car. Mostly, I jotted down points from the searchers. There's not much new, but you can see where we've looked already. If you want to come along, you could sit there and combine the information. It's not so cold this afternoon, but Richard has blankets in the back seat. Also, if you haven't eaten lunch, Mrs. Berkey brought several hampers with sandwiches along with flasks of hot tea and coffee."

"That was kind of her." She glanced at Jax and Jenkins. "I'll see you gentlemen later."

Jax watched her go with surprise. He had expected her to argue about not immediately joining the search.

"Have you eaten, son?" Jenkins asked, his voice breaking into Jax's thoughts.

Jax forced himself back to the present. "No, but I'm not hungry. I'll join the search now and have something later." After a glance at Bella, who had gone to Richard's car, Jax strode toward the fields and woods.

An hour later, Bella wrapped up her paperwork. Many of the teachers and students, not dressed for rough walking or gusty winds, had left after lunch. Among those who remained was Ida. She climbed into the car, grabbed a sandwich, and wrapped up with a blanket.

"Have you eaten?" Ida asked.

"No, but thanks for the reminder." When her stomach groaned, Bella laughed. "I hadn't realized how hungry I am." She took a sandwich before picking up one of the vacuum flasks. "There's still tea. Most of the coffee is gone."

"Tea sounds good," Ida replied. "It isn't as chilly as this morning, but the wind has picked up." She gratefully took a mug from Bella before going on. "Did you and Jax find anything helpful?"

"We discovered a lot," Bella replied before giving a recap of their morning and ending with Miss Crabtree's mechanic friend. "Do you know who he might be?"

Ida pursed her lips. "No, I've heard nothing about such a person. As I told you, Miss Crabtree kept to herself. She only spoke with the younger teachers in passing, and she wasn't close to any of the older teachers except Miss Lansing. It's possible she might know something about the man." Ida paused for a moment. "Miss Lansing was here earlier, but she and Mrs. Berkey returned to school shortly before you and Jax arrived. They want to answer telephone calls."

Bella frowned. "Are there usually a lot of calls during the day?"

Ida shook her head. "No, but a few came in early this morning. Word has gotten out about Miss Crabtree, and parents are concerned about a missing teacher. Naturally, they're worried about their daughters. I know Mrs. Berkey doesn't want to cancel classes for any length of time unless it's absolutely necessary, but it may come to that."

"Is she afraid people will permanently remove their girls?" Bella asked.

Ida's forehead furrowed as if in consternation. "She didn't actually say so, but I'm sure she must be. Boxmore Hill is rebounding in terms of enrollment. When I interviewed, board members said they hope to add back grades six and seven soon. That won't happen unless this case is solved quickly."

Bella replied without forethought. "Jax is trying really hard. He worked late last night, and he will again tonight because interviews are scheduled with the teachers."

A wide grin curved Ida's rosebud lips. "So, you and Jax must have gotten along well this morning."

Warmth rose in Bella's face at the implication in her friend's words and tone. "We got along fine." As soon as the statement was out, she realized her tone didn't match her words.

Ida's smile disappeared. "What happened?"

After a last bite of sandwich, Bella met her friend's worried gaze. "Nothing personal, if that's what you mean. He mentioned again that I need to listen when he thinks I might be in danger. After all, a brother would worry about me." Not his exact words, but they were the gist of his statement.

Whatever else the two friends might have said was interrupted by Nolen. "We're going to search one more area around here before we finish. Do you ladies want to come along, or would you rather go back to campus?"

Immediately, Bella replied, "I said I'd help, and I will."

Ida agreed and, as the pair moved out with the other searchers, she slipped her arm through Bella's. "Don't forget you have a sister," she murmured.

"I never do," Bella replied with a tremulous smile. A sister and a big brother, since Jax seemed to see that as his role in her life. Both thoughts should make her happy, but only one did. The other made her feel bereft, which was foolish. How could she miss something she'd never had? She and Jax had been friends for years, and he'd served as her escort at times. Before war loomed on the horizon, they'd been close to courting. Or so she'd thought. Now, Bella simply wished they could regain their old footing.

Sometime later, the search party had covered the designated area and found nothing new. By that time, Ida and Bella were among only a half-dozen teachers still in the field.

"A hot meal sounds good to me, but simply getting inside and warm will be wonderful," Ida observed.

"I agree. The temperature has dropped a lot since the sun started going down." Bella smiled at her friend, but her gaze went to where Jax was speaking with Nolen and Jenkins. "I should get going anyhow. Mrs. Berkey invited Jax for dinner before he interviews the teachers this evening."

"Do you suppose I can get a ride back with you?"

"Of course." When Jax joined them, Bella said, "Ida wants to ride to school with us."

A frown briefly creased his forehead before Jax carefully schooled his features. While walking the fields and woods, he'd had plenty of time to think, and most of his thoughts had centered on Bella. All afternoon he'd been reviewing their conversation and finding fault with himself. Why hadn't he revealed the truth about Matt's death sooner? Why was he waiting until the case ended? At the rate they were going, that wouldn't be soon. His deceit was a major impediment between them, but so was Griffith Biggins. Did Bella care for the golf pro? If she did, Jax would have to accept it. And, if she couldn't forgive him for his role in Matt's death, he'd have to accept that, too. At least, she had Biggins to offer support and solace. Even though Bella needed someone to care for her, and Mac wouldn't always be around, thinking about Biggins offering strength provided no relief. With those thoughts cascading through his head, Jax had planned to talk with her on the way back to school, but he could hardly reject Ida's request without appearing surly. "Of course," he replied. "I don't mind riding in back."

Bella opened her mouth, but Ida spoke before she had a chance. "That's nice of you, Jax. Thanks." She again took Bella's arm and hurried to the car, leaving Jax to follow in their wake.

Since he was relegated to the rear seat, Jax said little. Occasionally, he caught snatches of the conversation between Ida and Bella, but mostly he felt like the proverbial fifth wheel. When they got to school, he hurriedly climbed out. "How many interviews do we have this evening?"

"Twelve," Bella replied. "Mrs. Berkey gave me the list, and I organized them so that the new teachers are first."

"That sounds fine. One might know about the mechanic." He looked from Bella to Ida and back.

"I suppose you told Ida what we found out this morning."

A flush rose in Bella's cheeks, but she nodded. "I didn't think any of it was confidential."

"And I won't repeat it," Ida assured him.

"Please don't." Jax rubbed his jaw. "We've covered most of the ground around here. A car is very visible, yet we haven't found even a trace of it or of Miss Crabtree. It's mystifying, and I don't like that at all."

"Even Richard said it's a tough case, but some are more challenging than others. I know my grandfather said that often," Bella put in.

Before Jax could reply, Ida cleared her throat. "Bella said Mrs. Berkey invited you to eat at the teachers' table, Jax. Why don't you go ahead? Bella and I need to clean up a bit before dinner."

"Fine," he replied. "I'll see you in a little while."

The two friends said little as they headed to their room, but once they were inside, Ida closed the door and turned to Bella. "How could you spend hours together and discuss nothing personal?"

Bella bit her lower lip. "We briefly talked about him being upset with me last summer. I think I told you about it. On the way back from Cleveland, I asked why he didn't want a club pro job, which led to an unpleasant impasse. Jax was mad and said to mind my own business. Since we don't spend time together anymore, it hasn't been hard. This morning, I asked why he wanted me to help today, why he made it sound like I'd helped solve his other big cases, why he worked so hard to convince Mrs. Berkey that I should accompany him today and take notes this evening. I said he hadn't wanted my assistance in the past and made many excuses." She didn't delineate what they were since Ida already knew.

"How did he react?"

"He apologized and said he overreacted to me offering the job at Ballantyne and continuing to bring it up. He said I'm stronger than he is since I face the past and my losses every day."

Ida laid a hand on her friend's arm. "You are strong and persistent. I'm glad Jax sees that."

A tremulous smile touched Bella's mouth as she recalled his words. "He said he wished things were different, but wishing is futile."

Silence filled the room for a long moment. Finally, Ida spoke. "That sounds encouraging."

Her friend's predictable enthusiasm lifted Bella's spirits. "You're an eternal optimist, and you've already said you want us to have the happy ending you and Alan couldn't have."

For a moment, pain clouded Ida's hazel eyes. "I do. Losing Alan was a bitter pill, but I'm grateful for the time we had together."

"It isn't the same. You and Alan were engaged. Jax and I were childhood friends, and I had a girlish crush on him."

Ida put her hands on her hips. "By the time we left for France, you were past the crush stage." When

Bella started to deny the assertion, her friend hurried on. "We both know you were, and so was he. Jax didn't come to all of those college social functions because he thought of you as a little sister."

After moving from the desk chair to the edge of her bed, Bella tried to relax. "Jax came with Matt, so I would have an escort," she maintained, repeating what she'd told her friend more than once. She'd never admitted hoping for more because, like Jax, Bella had feared what the war would bring and hadn't thought too far ahead. "He was being a good friend. A big brother in some ways."

Ida pursed her lips and rolled her eyes. "Piffle. Jax doesn't look at you like a brother would."

As always, when her friend made such a remark, Bella's heart jumped with hope, but she forced herself to be calm. "Why would Jax say he wants to be a big brother if he doesn't? It makes no sense. Again, this morning, he said he worries about me." Part of her wanted to reveal her conflicting and persistent feelings but, even with her best friend, Bella maintained a core of privacy.

Ida gave Bella a long look. "A sweetheart would want you out of harm's way, too. As for the big brother bit, I don't know. He may still feel constrained by his friendship with Matt. Or he may worry about how much he's changed. After all, he's mentioned that more than once, hasn't he?"

"Yes, he's mentioned it several times," Bella agreed, "but we've all changed in some ways."

A shadow passed over Ida's face. "War does that."

Bella laid one hand on her friend's arm. "I'm so sorry. Of course, you know that better than anyone."

Her friend offered a weak smile. "But I would have felt equally sad if I had been here at home when Alan died. Jax is talking about experiences that changed him. You and I faced difficulties and circumstances that made us different, too. But we weren't on the front lines. We weren't in the trenches. We didn't have to send men into battle and watch them die. That had to take a heavy toll on him."

Briefly, Bella mulled over her friend's observations. "Yes, I'm sure it did. He still worries about the men in his platoon, and those in my brother's, too. He tries to help them."

"I'm sure he does." Ida paused. "On top of that, he was badly wounded himself. Dealing with physical injuries and emotional pain can't be easy. And there's his career change. He can't even play much golf, and it was his passion. You've also said he has a hard time being at Ballantyne because of the memories. I know your own memories must make it difficult for you, too." Her expression softened. "You can still play golf and, from what I saw last summer and fall, as well as you ever did. But Jax can't, can he?"

Bella clasped her hands in front of her and stared at them as she considered her friend's question. "I don't think so. He played nine holes a few times at Crystal Lakes last summer. Usually, late in the day when no one else was around." She glanced at Ida. "I've invited him to play Ballantyne, but he never has."

Again, Ida looked thoughtful. "If he doesn't play well, and how can he if driving and writing present problems, Jax most likely doesn't want you to know. Men don't like to be seen as weak, especially to a special girl. This big brother business is some sort of smoke screen. He always seemed a little shy to me, and he still does in some ways. When you combine that with his war experience, it could explain a lot. Give him more time, Bella."

For several moments, Bella pondered her friend's observation. Could Ida be right? Taking a wait and see approach would reveal nothing to Jax, so why not choose that route? For a little longer, she would. "I will."

Ida grinned. "Did you put me on the list of interviews for this evening?"

"I didn't, since I told Jax what you said." Bella chewed on her lower lip. "But he may want to talk with you himself."

"I'll run down and see if I can catch him alone while you change clothes."

The sudden change of topic confused Bella. "I'm planning to stay in the same clothes."

"You need to wear something more modern." As Bella was about to speak, Ida held up one hand. "No. We discussed your wardrobe last summer. Do this for me, if not for yourself. It won't take you long to change, and I'll go ahead."

Immediately, Bella's resistance ebbed. "Fine." Jax might see her as a little sister, or he might not. In either case, she didn't have to look frumpy.

Jax didn't immediately go to the dining hall. Instead, he looked around the campus for a while. The library was completely dark, so Miss Lansing must be at dinner. After stopping at the office and not finding Mrs. Ryerson, he headed to the cafeteria.

Giggling and chatter made Jax hesitate at the door. Heads turned and, while every eye might not have been on him, he felt highly scrutinized and very exposed. He licked his suddenly dry lips. What was wrong with him? He'd led men over the top and into No Man's Land. He could certainly enter a room filled with females. So, what if most were staring at him?

Before he moved forward, a voice sounded behind him. "Surveying the battlefield, lieutenant?"

A hot flush rose in his cheeks as he turned to face Ida. Amusement twinkled in her hazel eyes. He shrugged. "I know they're not adversaries," Jax replied. Ida's warm expression eased his mind. The woman was Bella's best friend and, like Mac, Ida supported and loved Bella. Those qualities endeared her to him.

"But entering a room filled with dozens of women and girls, all of whom are studying you like a specimen under glass, is a challenge," she suggested in a soft, teasing tone.

His cheeks burned hotter, but Jax nodded. "Yes, it is." He paused before asking, "Where is Bella? Is she all right?" They'd had a long day already, and he hoped she wasn't tired or chilled.

For a moment, Ida studied him. "I think so."

Concern filled Jax. "Is she ill?"

"No, not ill."

He shifted from one foot to the other. "Is something else wrong?"

"I don't know," Ida replied. "I'm a good listener, and I'm empathetic to your cause."

Jax frowned, but warmth once again surged into his face and he had trouble maintaining the woman's penetrating gaze. "I don't have a cause, except to find Miss Crabtree."

Ida pursed her lips and shook her head. "We both know that's not true. You've told Bella that you can be a big brother to her, but I suspect your feelings are not those of a sibling."

The stark statement set his heart to pounding so hard that Jax was afraid Ida could hear it. Hastily, he glanced away. "She told you about our conversation today, and probably about other discussions in the past." He wondered how much Ida knew. Most likely, a lot.

"Yes, she did," Ida replied. "Bella appreciated your apology, but she's upset about you treating her like a little sister, and I don't blame her."

His jaw tightened as Jax fought the urge to spill his heart out to Ida and ask for her help, but he couldn't do that. He needed to face Bella on his own. Once she realized the extent of his role in her brother's death, they could move forward...or not. "Long before now, I said Matt wanted me to look out for his family if something happened to him." He hadn't mentioned it again today, but Bella was aware of her brother's request, one Jax would have honored without being asked.

"Growing up, weren't you and Bella friends, too?" She didn't let him answer. "Do you see how you categorizing yourself as her brother's best friend and replacement might be hurtful?"

Amazement filled Jax as Ida's observation registered. "I never thought of it like that," he admitted. His efforts and subterfuge had been to protect Bella, not cause her additional pain.

Ida shoved her hands into her skirt pockets. "I don't know how much more I should say."

Jax searched Ida's troubled expression. "I don't want you to reveal Bella's confidences. She needs both you and Mac. She depends on you, and she might think telling me too much wasn't fair."

"You're a good man, Jax, but I have no idea what's holding you back." Ida's voice resonated with confusion. "No idea at all."

He shoved his hands into his pants pockets. "I don't know what you mean, Ida." Uneasiness filled him because he knew exactly what she meant. He hadn't realized he was so transparent, though.

She shook her head. "I think you do. I can't force you to tell me or Bella, either. Remember this, you can't expect her to wait forever. She's close to giving up on you now. Eventually, another man will come along and win her, even if she doesn't care for him as much as she does for you." Ida's voice held a firm note of certainty.

Dismay swept through Jax. What Ida said was undoubtedly true, and he admitted—to himself, at least—that the idea disturbed him. He planned to talk to Bella about Matt as soon as he could. But was he already too late? He swallowed convulsively over the emotions rising in his throat. The image of her laughing with Griffith Biggins hit him like a hammer blow. Only a short time ago, Jax had decided he could accept Bella caring for the other man. Ida's assertion tested that idea. Her light touch on his forearm drew his attention from his troubled thoughts into the present.

"There isn't anyone right now, if that's what worries you. I'm just saying there probably will be some day. Perhaps one day soon." Sadness filled her gaze. "I miss Alan terribly, but I treasure every moment we were together."

Her mention of her fiancé gave Jax pause. But her words hit him harder. Ida didn't know all about Alan Brewster, and he wouldn't be the one to tell her. "I'll give your words some thought after we find out what happened to Miss Crabtree." After the afternoon's search, he'd planned to talk with Bella on their way back to school. Now, Jax realized they needed an extended time when they wouldn't be interrupted, so it would have to wait until the case was solved. But no longer.

Ida nodded. "Bella didn't put me on this evening's interview list because she's already told you a lot of what I know. Do you have other questions?"

Jax forced personal ruminations from his mind and focused on the case. After reviewing what Bella had shared, he asked, "Is that all correct about Mrs. Ryerson, Miss Styles, and Miss Crabtree?"

"Yes, Bella got it right. I don't know Miss Styles, but I heard a lot of gossip when I started last fall. From all reports, she was terribly upset and angry with Miss Crabtree, and I can't blame her."

"Do you know if she was friendly with anyone here other than Mrs. Ryerson?"

"Dina is the only one in touch with her, so she may tell you more. A couple of teachers would have known Miss Styles years back. They could answer questions about how long Miss Styles and Miss Crabtree were at odds. They may also know more about Dina's school days and marriage. Bella made notations on the interviews schedule, so you'll know who the veteran teachers are."

As always, Bella was thorough. "Great, I'll..."

Abruptly, another voice cut through his. "Hello, constable. I'm scheduled to meet with you first. I'm Eliza Dobbs." One of the young teachers, a pert blonde, stopped next to Jax. "I've finished my supper, so we could talk any time."

Jax felt Ida's fingers tighten on his arm before she said, "The constable needs to eat dinner himself. If you'll excuse us, we want to go in."

"I believe the interviews start in thirty minutes," Jax said to the younger woman. "Miss Stewart and I will see you then."

Eliza's grin flattened, but she nodded. "Yes, of course. I'll use the time to freshen up." She turned and walked away.

"Thank you," he murmured as Ida dropped her hand, and they both moved forward.

"You're welcome. Remember, despite everything, I'm on your side." She paused for a heartbeat. "As long as you don't hurt Bella."

Chapter Seven

J AX HAD LITTLE APPETITE. Ida's comments about
Bella and his frustration with the investigation
combined to nag at him. The interviews might
prove useful, but physical evidence relating to the
woman's whereabouts was essential. Where was
she? With every passing hour, Jax felt his concern
grow, since the chance of finding Miss Crabtree
alive kept dwindling. When Bella came to the table,
his attention immediately traveled to her, although
she ignored the empty seat beside him and sat at
the opposite end.

"You're picking at your dinner," Ida murmured, so
that only he could hear. "And you're staring at Bella
with a forlorn expression."

Immediately, he glanced at Ida. "Thanks for
pointing that out," he replied in an equally quiet
voice, "and for sitting next to me." Jax lifted his fork
and stabbed a chunk of potato. Now wasn't the time

to think about his relationship, or lack thereof, with Bella. He needed to focus on the case.

Within moments, the headmistress was pulling back the chair next to him. Jax hurried to help her.

"Thank you, Constable Hastings," she said with a smile. "I hope you're enjoying your dinner."

"Yes, ma'am. It's kind of you to invite me." He couldn't have told her what he'd eaten because his mind had been elsewhere, but that wasn't the point.

"You've already had a long day, and you have a lengthy evening ahead of you here," she countered. "I'm sure you'll have work back at your office when you finally get there. Providing dinner for you is the least we can do."

"Thank you," he said again.

"I heard from some of those who helped with the search that nothing significant was found," Mrs. Berkey observed.

"I'm afraid that's right. No sign of Miss Crabtree or her vehicle."

"Dare I hope you uncovered something helpful during your travels today?" When Jax hesitated, she hurried on. "I'm not asking for detailed information. I suppose I'm hoping something positive has turned up. We've gotten calls from parents, and they're concerned about their daughters."

"We have information that may or may not prove useful. I'm hoping some teachers can flesh it out for us in this evening's interviews," he told her. "As far as parental concerns, there's nothing to indicate someone is targeting the faculty or students here. Miss Crabtree didn't make it back to school. She was last seen in Boxwood, which isn't far, but, as

I said, there's no sign of her or the car near the roads from there to here. If she'd gone missing from campus, I'd worry about a threat to your pupils and teachers." He looked up and down the table. Some instructors were close enough to overhear, and Jax didn't want gossip spreading, so he kept his voice hushed. "I can give you more details later, if that's all right."

"Of course. Later is fine. It's good to know you got information," the headmistress said, "but parents worry. Some came today to pick up their girls, and more will be here tomorrow. Due to that, I'm canceling our weekend activities and classes on Monday."

Tension knotted Jax's insides. He laid his fork down. "I'm sorry, Mrs. Berkey, but we're doing our best. With luck, more leads will develop." The very near future was his hope.

"I know you're doing what you can, constable. I really hope you solve this case soon. Boxmore Hill is getting re-established, as you probably know. Having a teacher come up missing on her way back here is very troubling."

"Yes, ma'am," he agreed. "If you like, I can meet with you after the interviews. I'll provide more details, and you can ask questions."

A slight smile touched her lips. "You haven't seen the schedule set up by Miss Stewart. She put me last. We can talk then." She glanced at the watch pinned to her lapel. "You still have a few minutes before your first interview, so I'll let you eat the rest of your dinner in peace."

A BAFFLING ABSENCE

Jax tried to finish his meal but, as soon as Bella rose from her chair, he hastily excused himself and hurried to join her. After catching up, he schooled his features into what he hoped was an amiable expression. "Are you ready for the interviews?" His conversation with Ida left him feeling ill at ease, so did the case and Mrs. Berkey's concern. Pressure kept building, which made maintaining a calm demeanor difficult.

"Of course," she said. "We're using a room near the office. The first interview is in ten minutes, so we should go, if you're set."

"I am." He followed Bella into the main hall. Once he was next to her, Jax gently touched her elbow. Abruptly, she stopped and glanced at him.

"Yes." Her tentative tone telegraphed confusion.

A rough sigh escaped him. "You look very nice this evening." His words sounded stilted, but her lips softened into a grin, and Jax relaxed.

"Thank you." Color suffused her cheeks. "This outfit belongs to Ida. I didn't bring many things with me, and I was dusty from being out all day." She glanced away. "We should get going. We don't want to be late."

Jax followed her to the conference room and sat down next to her at the long table. Once again, he moved his thoughts to the investigation. "Who is first on your list?"

"Eliza Dobbs," Bella replied before ushering the young teacher into the room.

"Good evening," Miss Dobbs said, beaming at him.

Jax replied as he got to his feet and held the chair for Eliza, who focused her attention solely on him. He didn't smile back.

"Why thank you, constable. You're such a gentleman."

Jax merely nodded in response. She was the one who had accosted him outside the dining room. "Thank you for taking time to speak with us."

"I want to do whatever I can to be of assistance. We're all distraught over Miss Crabtree being missing," Eliza said.

"From what Mrs. Berkey told me, you are new to the school. I believe you started last fall, is that right?" Jax asked in a pleasant, but professional, voice.

"That's right," Eliza replied. "But I was a student here, too."

"When did you finish?" Jax asked.

"May 1917. I attended college after that. My parents had promised me a trip to France when I graduated, but the war got in the way. I was very disappointed. A friend was there last summer, but she didn't have a good time. She said the countryside is a mess and even Paris isn't ideal." Her lips went flat.

Her expression and tone clearly indicated Eliza found this to be a personal affront. Jax, hands clenching, fought against chastising the girl, who deserved to be upbraided, in his opinion. Memories of the battered French landscape remained vivid. His emotions raw, he tried to focus on the investigation, not on correcting some foolish young thing.

When Bella responded, she showed no such compunction. "Most of the soldiers didn't have a good time, either. Especially the ones who never got home. Of course, the French people didn't find the war to be ideal themselves, nor did the Belgians."

The judgmental edge in Bella's voice was clear to Jax, and he was glad she'd taken the girl to task. A teacher ought to have some knowledge of the recent war and its horrific consequences.

Eliza looked blankly at Bella before turning back to Jax. Her flirty grin re-emerged. "I almost forgot that you were a war hero, constable."

Jax's tension spread from his clenched hands to his square jaw, where a muscle twitched spasmodically. "I was no hero," he ground out. "Now, if we can get back to Miss Crabtree. Were you ever in any of her classes?"

The flirty smile became a childish pout, but the young teacher replied, "Oh, yes. Every year. She expected a lot from her students, and her classes weren't very interesting. Most of us girls thought she was well-named." When Jax simply stared at her, she continued. "You know. Crabtree. Crabby."

Although Eliza grinned at her little joke, it fell flat. Jax shook his head. So much for her feeling distraught. Had the girl's parents given money to the school, or was Boxmore Hill desperate for teachers? "So, you weren't close to Miss Crabtree?"

A humorless laugh escaped Eliza. "She wasn't close to anyone except Fancy Fanny, who is as dull and demanding as Crabby."

"Are you talking about Miss Lansing and Miss Crabtree?" Again, Bella's tone revealed disapproval.

Eliza barely spared her a glance. "When I was a student, we used those nicknames for them. Some of the younger teachers do, as well. You know why Crabby fits. Fanny is Miss Lansing's given name and Fancy...she's the exact opposite." When neither Jax nor Bella replied, the young teacher continued. "Neither of them liked me when I was a student, and they weren't happy when I was hired here. I try to be pleasant, but they barely speak to me." A little huffing breath left her. "Except to berate me."

"Why would they do that?" Several possibilities came to Jax's mind.

"I took one of my classes to the library for research," the young teacher replied. "My students were all busy, so I wandered around. Miss Lansing and Miss Crabtree were in the office talking. I was looking at books near the open door and couldn't help but overhear them. They mentioned getting auto repairs done by a friend who lives in the area. They were saying how he didn't charge nearly as much as other places around here, so I was interested since my Roamer roadster was acting up. I didn't interrupt or anything." She rolled her eyes. "I knew better. Later, I asked Miss Lansing where she took her car. She said to a friend, but when I asked where he was, she insisted he was too busy to take any new customers."

Jax straightened in his chair at this dribble of news. "Did she mention his name?"

"I overheard them say *Andy*, but Miss Lansing said to mind my own business, which should have been helping my students, not listening to private conversations. Later, I asked Miss Crabtree. She wouldn't give me details because she didn't want me bothering him, like I'd do that." Again, the girl huffed, as if disgusted.

Jax focused on the name. "Did Miss Crabtree use his name?"

Eliza shrugged. "I think she said *Andy*, but I don't remember for sure. She hurried off, and I finally took my Roamer to a mechanic in Toledo when two other teachers and I drove up there to shop and such. Life is dull here, and we can't get away often at all." She paused briefly. "I thought working would give me more independence since my parents are so old-fashioned. But there are more rules here than at home, and it's a lot harder to sneak out. And no fun places to go nearby, either."

Jax ignored her chatter and focused on potential evidence. "So, you don't have any idea where this friend is located."

Eliza's brow furrowed. "From what I overheard in the library, he must be about a half-hour away."

"Do you know if he has a garage or works from his home?" They already knew the mechanic was about fifteen to twenty minutes northeast of Boxwood. Knowing he was thirty minutes from the school made Jax draw a mental map in his mind. That hardly enabled him to pinpoint a location, so he still needed details, and Miss Lansing should be able to provide them.

"No, I don't." Her blue gaze narrowed on Jax. "Why? Is that important?"

Hurriedly, Jax shook his head. "No, not really. I was only curious." He didn't want the girl parroting his words and spreading speculation, so he quickly wrapped up the interview and rose to his feet. "Again, thank you for your time."

"I'm happy to help you, constable. Is there anything else I can do?" she asked, remaining in her chair.

"No, you're free to go," Jax said with a note of finality.

Eliza frowned, but she rose as Jax again held the chair. "You know where to find me if you want anything," she said before leaving the room without a word or glance for Bella.

Jax sat down again. "The girl is immature and spoiled. She seems more suited to attending parties than teaching school. Her parents must have money since she was a student here, and she expected a trip to Europe after graduation. Not to mention, she drives a Roamer roadster. Those aren't cheap."

"I imagine she comes from an affluent family. Most students do." Bella shook her head. "She should set a good example instead of breaking the rules, though. If Mrs. Berkey knew about Eliza sneaking out, she'd be appalled."

He grinned again. "I bet she'd be appalled at whatever Eliza and her friends do in Toledo, too. I'm guessing they found a speakeasy, which wouldn't be all that hard."

Bella's gaze narrowed on him. "How do you know about speakeasies in the city?"

A shrug lifted his good shoulder. "I'm a constable. I hear things."

"I'm sure you do." She paused briefly. "Do you know about liquor being sold around here?"

He shook his head. "Certainly not within my jurisdiction. It's more likely people are making booze at home. I'm sure some do. If they drink it themselves on their own property, I may not hear about it. And that's not illegal. If they sold the stuff, that would be a problem I'd need to address." Not that Jax currently needed more crimes to handle. "Illegal distribution of homemade liquor usually brings other issues with it. Being so close to Lake Erie, the stuff sometimes comes in from Canada, but prohibition agents are charged with controlling illegal imports, not town constables. Some locals are empowered to investigate problems in their areas. So far, we haven't been."

"We never served liquor at the resort, but people brought their own with them. I wonder if they still do."

Hearing the anxiety in her words, Jax offered reassurance. "It's possible, but don't worry about it. If it becomes a big issue, I'll hear and handle it. You and Mac wouldn't be responsible for your guests having booze in their cottages, rooms, or any place on the property."

"All right," Bella replied.

He nodded. "Right now, I need to solve Miss Crabtree's disappearance. From what we've learned so far, I have a little better idea of where the mechanic is. Who is next on your list?"

Bella scanned the paper and provided names. "Miss Lansing is later. Right before Mrs. Ryerson."

"We'll definitely ask Miss Lansing about the friend who works on cars. Like I told you, she wasn't forthcoming when I talked to her. She never mentioned the mechanic friend, which seems odd now."

"I agree, but I can see Eliza being a pest. They might not have told her about the man due to that."

"You think she'd be a pest?" Jax asked, but he couldn't keep amusement from his voice. When Bella laughed, he chuckled along with her. "The girl can't be much younger than I am. Probably a few years' difference, but she made me feel really old."

"I doubt if that was her intention," Bella said, before hurrying on. "Our next interview should be here. I'll check."

As Jax watched Bella leave, he realized she'd noted Eliza's flirtatious manner. Was she jealous? The possibility was more encouraging than it should have been.

The next bunch of teachers had no new information, which added to Jax's frustration. "Miss Lansing should be next, right?"

A tap on the door interrupted, and Mrs. Berkey poked her head in. "I don't want to disturb you, but I wondered if you need anything. Some hot tea, perhaps?"

Both Jax and Bella turned the offer down, but he rose and waved the headmistress into the room. "Sit down for a moment, ma'am."

Mrs. Berkey perched on the nearest chair. "Can I help you with something?"

"We've heard that Miss Lansing and Miss Crabtree took their automobiles to a friend living about thirty minutes from here. We already found out she planned to stop there after leaving Boxwood, but we don't know the man's name or exact location. Evidently, they referred to him as Andy."

Mrs. Berkey's eyes widened. "Mr. Andy Anderson was the groundskeeper here for many years. He left before I arrived, and I didn't know he worked on vehicles or where he moved. Miss Crabtree was always interested in the grounds and how they looked. They collaborated on planning the library's garden. We're all quite proud of our park-like setting," she observed with a smile.

Bella paused in her note-taking to say, "It's a beautiful campus."

The older woman sent a grateful look her way. "Having been raised and still living at Ballantyne, you would appreciate natural beauty." Mrs. Berkey looked back at Jax. "I'm sure you do, too, constable."

"Yes, the campus is a lovely place." He cleared his throat. "Do you know why Mr. Anderson left?"

The headmistress glanced down at the table. "He came into a small inheritance and bought a place of his own. Enrollment had fallen dramatically at that point, and the faculty and staff thought Boxmore Hill might close. I believe that was a major concern for him."

"It seems like he might have waited to see if enrollment picked up again, especially if he only received a small sum of money. Do you know if there were other reasons for him to leave?" Jax watched the woman closely.

Mrs. Berkey clasped her hands together more tightly. "I dislike repeating gossip."

The woman apparently had information, but was hesitant to reveal it. "I understand," Jax readily agreed, "but we need every detail we can get. Time is crucial in a missing person case. I wouldn't ask you to repeat hearsay otherwise."

Slowly, she met his gaze and nodded. "The gossip is that Mr. Anderson was fired. Miss Lansing and Miss Crabtree cite some sort of inheritance as his reason for leaving. Most others say he was not always using his work hours effectively."

Her statements, while carefully worded, provided fresh details. Since Ida hadn't heard this speculation, Bella wondered if it was only a topic among the older faculty members. As silence ensued, she figured Jax was considering how to proceed. Tainting Mrs. Berkey's statements by offering tidbits about their knowledge of the Ryerson-Crabtree rivalry wouldn't lead to any genuine clues. Perhaps, a more general observation might. "You mean he was wasting time? Or was he leaving campus when he should have been working?" she asked.

Color suffused the headmistress' cheeks. "He seemed to spend a good deal of time in the library."

Jax caught Bella's gaze when he looked at her again. She seemed as surprised as he felt.

"Do you have any idea why?" he asked.

Mrs. Berkey shook her gray head. "I will not conjecture, constable, and I do not know if the rumors are true. If he spent time there, I sincerely doubt it was for any—uh—well, for any clandestine purpose, as some have suggested."

"I'm not asking for speculation, ma'am. But we have a missing teacher, and no factual evidence on her whereabouts. My team and I are working as hard as we can, and I need as much information as possible in order to find her." Jax paused momentarily. "I know you want that, too."

The headmistress braced her elbows on the table and put her head in her hands. "Of course, I do." When she looked up, her face was a mask of dismay. "Some of the long-time teachers suggest that Mr. Anderson and Miss Lansing were friendly. Too friendly. I don't know if that was true or not, and I haven't engaged in tittle-tattle on the subject."

"I understand," Jax said. "We won't, either."

"Thank you," the headmistress replied. "As you know, Miss Crabtree and Miss Lansing are friendly with each other, but not with others on staff. I believe there is resentment for that reason."

"Understandable," Jax said. "I also wondered about Mrs. Ryerson's relationship with Miss Crabtree. I'm not asking you to engage in hearsay, but we've heard they never got along."

The tension drained from Mrs. Berkey's shoulders. "That would be a fair statement. Dina can tell you far more, but my understanding is the two of them competed when they were students. I believe they started as friends, but time and circumstances changed that. Loretta's personality is not as—let's say, pleasing—as Dina's. Nor is she as attractive. Even though they were well-matched academically, Dina was a leader while Loretta had few friends, from what I know. It seems to be common knowledge among the older teachers. As for now, Loretta still has few friends, which you already know. I'm sorry I didn't mention Mr. Anderson as one of them, but I wasn't aware of him working on her car. In fact, I didn't know he was close enough to Boxmore Hill to do such services for her. I only heard they were friendly when he was here."

Jax nodded. "I understand. It seems only a handful of people knew about him remaining in the area."

The headmistress pursed her lips. "That doesn't surprise me. Miss Lansing and Miss Crabtree are close. Neither of them has much to do with the other teachers, which can cause difficulties. They tolerate those who defer to them and sometimes help the ones who exhibit due respect."

"Interesting," Jax agreed before returning to his question and making it more pointed. "Do you think Mrs. Ryerson has hard feelings toward Miss Crabtree?"

A frown formed on Mrs. Berkey's face. "Miss Crabtree has not been kind to Dina. She criticized her choice of husband. That was when they were still in school. I believe Dina was deeply in love with Mr. Ryerson. Even though her parents disowned her when she wed, I don't believe she regrets marrying him. Quite the contrary, as far as I know. Dina is glad they had those years together." She released a pent-up breath. "Loretta hasn't a shred of sympathy for Dina's situation. She's made cutting remarks to others about it in Dina's presence, and she's flaunted her own fortune. I spoke to Loretta, but she has the upper hand because of her family's trust. It still provides funds for the school, and she has control over it." The headmistress paused. "At dinner, you said you learned some things this morning."

He quickly summarized the information. "I didn't want to say at the table since I feared being overheard. Plus, I didn't want to color your observations. We have a number of details, and several potential suspects, but nothing leads us to anyone in particular. Not yet, at least."

The color ebbed from the headmistress's face. "You can't possibly suspect Dina. Or Miss Styles."

"We spoke with Grover Hilliard. He and Miss Crabtree argued after dinner on Friday. Several people overheard them," Jax said, providing another bit of insight.

The older woman's eyes widened. "I don't know Mr. Hilliard well. He's been here to take photographs, and I've briefly spoken with him. This morning, he stopped on his way back home. He wanted to speak with Dina about scheduling sittings for our club photographs. I didn't see him since it was during chapel, but he was terribly upset when he found out about Loretta being absent, according to Dina."

The revelations surprised Jax since Hilliard hadn't mentioned being at the school. "Wasn't Mrs. Ryerson at chapel?"

"Not this morning. We got several telephone calls early, and I didn't want to leave the office unattended," Mrs. Berkey said.

"So, Mr. Hilliard spoke with Mrs. Ryerson," Bella said, "and she told him about Miss Crabtree."

The headmistress nodded. "Yes. That's what I just said."

"You've surely heard about Miss Crabtree and Mr. Hilliard meeting in Boxwood," Jax said.

"Some, but it isn't common knowledge on campus," Mrs. Berkey admitted. "Dina mentioned seeing them, and she shared about them being acquainted years ago. I don't know details. As I've already told you, Miss Crabtree is a very private person."

Jax wondered if Mrs. Ryerson had done more than mention seeing the pair. And he wondered if she'd told others. That seemed likely. Now, more than ever, Jax wanted to speak with Dina Ryerson. Since he didn't need to say so again, Jax latched on to the headmistress's last statement. "Miss Crabtree's desire for privacy makes it more difficult to follow her trail." The benign remark revealed nothing, which was his intention. Discussing potential suspects with the headmistress was a poor strategy, especially since she seemed fond of at least one.

"This is becoming more and more confusing," Mrs. Berkey said. "I was hoping you'd quickly find Loretta."

"I did, too, ma'am." Jax drummed his fingers on the table. "As far as Miss Crabtree, has she ever threatened to stop donating to the school?"

The headmistress nodded. "She has. That puts me in a precarious position as far as supporting Dina. I have advised her to ignore Loretta as best she can."

"Has Mrs. Ryerson taken heed of your counsel?" Jax inquired.

Mrs. Berkey studied her clasped hands as if the answer might be found in them. When she finally spoke, her voice was subdued. "In some ways, yes. However, she made any request from Miss Crabtree a very low priority."

"Did that anger Miss Crabtree?" Jax asked.

The older woman released a long breath. "Loretta wasn't happy, and I discussed it with both of them on several occasions."

"Did they come to an understanding?" Jax doubted that was the case.

"I'm sorry to say they didn't." Mrs. Berkey massaged her temples with her forefingers, but her expression remained taut with tension. "They had words again before Easter vacation. Unfortunately, several students overheard them and another faculty member did, as well. I spoke with Dina and Loretta together, but it didn't help much. Loretta was adamant about Dina doing her job or being fired. She said if I wouldn't deal with the issue, she would go to the board."

Bella and Jax exchanged glances before he spoke again. They knew she'd done that with Miss Styles. "What did Mrs. Ryerson say?" he asked.

"Very little while Loretta was in the room. Afterward, she cried because she desperately needs this job. I told her again she should stop pushing Loretta's work requests to the side, but Dina was anxious about Loretta contacting board members right after the Easter holiday. I tried to reassure Dina. Of course, I couldn't say Loretta wouldn't go ahead with her threat. However, I spoke with her again before she left campus, and I urged her not to do that."

"Do you know if Miss Crabtree called any board members while she was away?" Jax inquired.

"No, I don't. I have received no calls, but Loretta's disappearance has been foremost in the minds of our staff, students, parents, alumni, and board members in the past few days. I can't be certain that she didn't contact one or more of them. I haven't heard from anyone on the subject, though."

"That's understandable," Jax told her. No one would hurry to dismiss an employee under the current circumstances.

A knock on the door again broke in. Bella rose to open it. "Miss Lansing, we'll be right with you."

"I have some paperwork to do, but I'll remain in the office until you wrap up, constable." Mrs. Berkey nodded to Bella before leaving the room.

The librarian appeared a moment later. As he had with each woman, Jax got to his feet. "Thank you for speaking with us, ma'am."

"Of course. I'm more than willing to assist in any way I can. Loretta, that is, Miss Crabtree was a good friend." The librarian paused for a moment as she focused on Jax. "She was rather eccentric, but we all have our idiosyncrasies."

Jax, who immediately noticed the use of past tense, peeked at Bella. Her rounded eyes telegraphed the certainty that she'd noticed, too. "When you say she was eccentric, what exactly do you mean?" he asked.

Miss Lansing patted the cameo brooch at the collar of her starched white blouse. "I'm sure you've been told she almost always returned late from her travels."

"Yes, I've heard that," Jax agreed. When Lansing said nothing more, he continued. "In what other ways would you say she was eccentric?"

Her fingers fluttered against the pin. "Loretta was very set in her ways, but I suppose many of us get that way as we grow older, especially those of us who are spinsters." Her gaze flickered to Bella before returning to Jax. "She had her own way of doing things, and she was very independent. Most women our age would hesitate to travel alone, but Loretta felt no compunction about doing so. I often warned her to be careful, but she drove to the train station in Toledo and went on to Minneapolis by herself. Sometimes, she drove up to Toledo to shop, as well. By herself." Lansing shook her head. "I wish she had taken more precautions. Going to big cities can be quite dangerous."

"Miss Crabtree was seen in Boxwood late on Friday afternoon, so she was almost back to school, not in a big city or a strange place," Jax said.

Miss Lansing's fingers stilled on the pin. For a moment, she sat as if frozen in place. Finally, her gaunt features relaxed into the semblance of a smile. "Of course, but what if someone followed her from Toledo? The last leg of the trip is on a relatively quiet road. When I've gone to Boxwood, I've driven it myself, and I rarely see another vehicle."

"How often do you go to Boxwood?" Jax asked.

"Not very often at all," she replied in a rather huffy tone. "I am busy here at school. Occasionally, Loretta and I have gone to the diner for a meal and

153

to a store for a few items. Nothing more, and that was prior to last fall."

The comment opened an avenue to discuss Hilliard. "Because she began seeing Grover Hilliard again." Jax made it a statement and watched for the woman's response.

The librarian's eyes widened before she carefully composed her features. "They never stepped out, as far as I know. Certainly not as anything more than friendly acquaintances. I believe he was sweet on her years ago when Loretta was a student, but he was angling above his station."

The last remark made Jax wonder if Lansing was as snobbish as Crabtree. "Mr. Hilliard is an accomplished photographer and has been for many years."

"His background is common," the woman said in a dismissive tone.

Possibly, Lansing was worse than Crabtree. Since he wasn't learning anything new about Hilliard from her, Jax took a roundabout way to discuss Anderson. "Do you also go to Boxwood to get work done on your vehicle? There's a filling station."

A moment of hesitation preceded the woman's response. "No, I do not take my car there for repair."

When she didn't expand on the answer, Jax continued, "You have a friend who works on it?"

Lansing's eyes blinked as if she was trying to clear her vision. At the same time, she laid both hands in her lap. Yet, her expression never changed, nor did her tone. "Why, yes, I have an old friend who likes to tinker with vehicles. His rates are quite modest, so I take my car there when it needs any sort of work."

"I understand he once was employed here." Jax's voice also remained calm.

The librarian glanced away before shifting in her chair, as if trying to get comfortable. "Yes, Mr. Anderson was the groundskeeper for many years. He not only has a love of gardens, he is quite enthralled with vehicles. He bought one early on and learned much from working on it. Now, he enjoys helping others when they have car trouble. Or to maintain the vehicles properly."

"I see," Jax said. "And Miss Crabtree also took her car to him. I suppose she was acquainted with Mr. Anderson when he worked here."

"Mr. Anderson began his employment at Boxmore Hill when Loretta and I were students." A smile touched her lips but not her eyes. "We were all much younger back then."

"Since all of you were long-time friends, you must know why Mr. Anderson left Boxmore Hill," Jax suggested. His attention moved to Bella, who was riveted on the librarian, while her pencil point remained on the notepad.

The librarian folded her hands on the table. "He came into a small inheritance from an uncle. Enrollment had fallen, and none of us was sure that Boxmore would survive." Her benign, faint smile appeared again. "Luckily, it has, but Mr. Anderson could make a change, so he did."

"Do you see him often?" Jax asked.

A shrug lifted one of the woman's bony shoulders. "Occasionally. Why so many questions about Mr. Anderson? He is no longer part of our campus community."

Jax leaned back in his chair and studied the librarian. "We understand he lives close to here, and I wondered if Miss Crabtree might have stopped to see him on her way back to school." He knew she'd planned to do so. Did Lansing know, too?

"I doubt that very much," the older woman hurried to say. "There would be no reason for her to go there. She would have been eager to get back to school, I'm sure."

Since the observation was at odds with Miss Crabtree frequently being late, Jax tucked it away for future reference. "Perhaps, she ran into car trouble and wanted him to look at her vehicle. How close is his home to Boxwood?" He knew the answer, but wanted to hear more from the librarian.

Miss Lansing sat up straighter. "About fifteen or twenty minutes from there, I believe. It wouldn't be on her way back here, though. It's more northeast of the town."

Again, Jax noted the information and how it connected with what they'd already learned. The woman was more forthcoming than when he'd previously spoken with her. But he had sharper questions now. There were plenty of puzzle pieces to put in place. After the interviews, he hoped to sort out some with Bella. "But if she had car trouble, Miss Crabtree might have gone out of her way to have Mr. Anderson look at it, don't you think?"

"It's possible, but Mr. Anderson visited a cousin last weekend, so he would not have been at home even if Loretta stopped," the librarian said. "He left at noon on Friday and didn't plan to get home until later tomorrow."

"That's six days, which seems like a long time to be away. Perhaps he returned early. Could she have called him from Boxwood?" Jax continued to make his inquiries in a calm, casual voice, but he found her in-depth knowledge of the man's travels intriguing.

"No, he doesn't have a telephone." Lansing paused before continuing. "I suppose she could have gone to his house if the car was misbehaving, although, as I say, it would have taken her out of her way, and she would not have found him there. I seriously doubt he would have returned early. Mr. Anderson lives a long way out with no neighbors nearby. If someone was following Loretta..." Her voice grew ragged before trailing off. She put her face in her hands.

Bella and Jax exchanged a look before he spoke again. "I'm sorry if I've upset you, Miss Lansing. I know it must be difficult to have your friend missing. Please believe me when I say, we're doing everything we can to find her."

The older woman lifted her head. Her expression was stricken, but her eyes were dry. "Thank you, constable," she said in a low whisper. "It is terribly disturbing. I hate to think of what could have happened to her."

"Yes, it is," he replied before continuing. "You can help us by giving me Mr. Anderson's location. I'd like to speak with him."

Her eyes widened. "Why? I told you he was gone last weekend and probably still is. He wouldn't know anything."

"I want to cover all the bases, and I know you want to help in any way you can." Jax offered a reassuring grin. "Besides, as you say, someone could have followed Miss Crabtree from Boxwood to his place. If that happened, and she was alone there..." Jax let his voice trail off. The scenario seemed unlikely, but he needed the location of Anderson's home. As protective of him as Lansing seemed, Jax didn't want an open confrontation. Most likely, she knew nothing about her friend's disappearance. But he wasn't ruling out anyone yet.

"I don't think he'll be able to help you, but I know he'll try. Mr. Anderson is a good man." She paused for a moment. "Have you spoken with Mrs. Ryerson yet?"

Jax's brow furrowed as he looked back at Bella, who was studying the librarian. "Not yet."

"Why do you ask, Miss Lansing?" Jax inquired.

"I don't want to carry tales," she began in a soft voice. "But Mrs. Ryerson and Loretta never got along. Dina, Mrs. Ryerson, always envied Loretta, but her antipathy has been much worse since she took the job as school secretary."

"Were all of you in the same class?" Jax inquired rather than revealing any clues.

"Yes, we were." Miss Lansing pursed her lips as if in distaste. "Dina's parents were very wealthy, and they spoiled her terribly. She had to have the best of everything. She flaunted her clothes and such."

"Weren't Miss Crabtree's parents wealthy, too?" he asked, knowing they had been.

158

"Yes, but Loretta didn't care about clothes," Lansing told Jax. "You haven't met her, and I don't know if you have seen a photograph or not."

"Mrs. Berkey gave a framed photograph to me. A portrait." They'd needed something in case the body, not the woman, was found.

"Then, you could see that she's not a beauty," Miss Lansing said. "She never was. Loretta was a gangly girl, while Dina was a pretty little thing, much like now, but with a sugary demeanor that garnered male attention. She's the same now. Both were smart, and they often vied for academic awards and class offices. Those were the original sources of conflict between them."

"Why do they still not get along? They've been out of school a long time, so I'd think they could put their rivalry behind them." Jax knew the source of their animosity, but he wanted to hear it from the librarian.

Lansing shrugged. "Loretta was very open about how foolish Dina was to marry without her parents' consent and be disinherited." Her voice hushed, making it seem as if she was revealing a confidence. "Dina's husband was a ne'er-do-well, but a handsome and charming one. He taught art here. When the board members discovered he'd been courting a student, he was fired. Even so, Dina married him shortly after graduation, and her parents cut her off." The librarian tut-tutted as if chastising a child. "Very short-sighted of her. The husband had talent, but hardly enough to make a living as an artist. Then, he got ill and died. Left her without a dollar. That's what brought Dina back here."

159

"Miss Crabtree has continued to make her opinion of Mrs. Ryerson's marriage clear?" Jax kept his gaze on the librarian, reading her expression as much as her words. He wanted to confirm what they'd already learned and, with luck, get additional details.

"I'm afraid she did. That made Dina angry, and they had words a few times. Dina also ignored Loretta's requests. Some teachers rely on the school secretary to type items for them, and for other clerical duties. More than once, Dina lost or forgot Loretta's work." Lansing paused as if to let the revelations sink in. "Loretta spoke with Mrs. Berkey shortly before Easter. She wanted Dina fired."

"I see," Jax murmured. "Do you know if Mrs. Berkey planned to dismiss Mrs. Ryerson?"

The librarian shrugged. "Loretta said our headmistress would take it under consideration, but I doubt if the woman did anything. Mrs. Berkey is a lackluster leader. Loretta would have needed to go over her head to get action."

"How would she go about that? Taking action, I mean," Jax said.

The older woman stared at him as if he was a dolt. "Constable, a headmistress reports to the board of trustees. Since Loretta had ample influence, she could have contacted each of them directly."

The librarian's terse tone made it sound like she was berating a foolish schoolboy, but Jax was no kid. She could say whatever she wanted, and he'd put up with her attitude to get information. "Isn't that what she did to get Miss Styles fired?"

Miss Lansing stiffened. For a moment, she simply stared into space. When she looked back at Jax, the mask of composure was once again in place. "Miss Styles was even worse than Dina. She criticized Loretta frequently. That was imprudent."

Jax couldn't deny the assertion. With no further questions, he wrapped up the interview. Since the woman had neatly side-stepped his request for the former groundskeeper's place of residence, he made it again. "I still need directions to Mr. Anderson's home. If you'd jot them down, I'd be grateful." The librarian hesitated long enough that Jax felt his uneasiness about her growing. "Bella, why don't you give Miss Lansing a slip of paper and let her borrow your pencil."

"I have paper and pencil." The older woman dug into her pocketbook, extracted the items, made a note, and handed it to Jax. "Here you are."

"Thank you." Jax got to his feet. "You've been a big help, ma'am. We appreciate your time."

Miss Lansing sighed. Once again, dismay stamped her face. "Of course. I hope I have been useful. I worry about Loretta."

Chapter Eight

AFTER THE LIBRARIAN LEFT, Jax turned to Bella. "There's a lot to discuss, and I want to get your opinion, but we're already running late. I hope you won't mind spending a few minutes reviewing the interviews after we finish."

Bella considered his observations. "Not at all. We've gotten more details to go over."

"Now, something to link them together would be useful." Jax braced his elbows on the table. "I talked to the custodian, groundskeeper, and cook earlier. They didn't have any information. None lives on campus, and they weren't here over the holiday break. The housemother in the student dormitory didn't arrive back until Tuesday morning, and she knew nothing of importance, either."

"How are you going to ask about Miss Crabtree's criticism of Mrs. Ryerson, especially about her marriage? Questions along those lines are likely to upset her, even if she had nothing to do with the disappearance."

He ran his fingers through his hair. "I'm not sure. It has to be a sore subject, especially since her husband died. I'll probably begin with some general questions. If you see an opportunity to ask something more personal, go ahead."

She considered the situation. "All right. Do you want me to see if Mrs. Ryerson is here?" Bella flexed her hand as she spoke. She'd taken a number of notes, and her fingers ached from gripping the pencil. And probably from tension. Her mind was whirling, and she figured Jax must have the same issue. They'd learned a lot, but analyzing it to move the case forward would be a challenge.

"Please do."

Bella left the room but came back alone. "She isn't at her desk, but Mrs. Berkey is still here. She hasn't seen Mrs. Ryerson since dinner."

Jax frowned. "That's odd. She knew what time to be back, didn't she?"

"Yes, she did. In fact, she asked again at dinner, and I confirmed it for her."

"Did she seem hesitant to meet with us?"

"Not that I noticed," Bella replied. Her thoughts returned to their last exchange. "She seemed the same as always. Pleasant and polite. When I last saw her, I didn't note any sign that Mrs. Ryerson wasn't perfectly ready and willing to be interviewed."

"There could be a reasonable explanation, I suppose."

A light tap on the door interrupted their conversation. Jax stood up as Mrs. Berkey entered the room. "I don't know what happened to Dina," the woman said. "I called the front desk at the faculty residence. The teachers take turns answering it in the evening, since that's when personal calls come in. Miss Dobbs is on duty right now but hasn't seen Dina. It isn't like her to miss a meeting or appointment." She clasped her hands together. "Dina looked worn out this afternoon. Perhaps, she planned to lie down before her interview and she fell asleep." The headmistress absently played with the gold band on her left hand as she spoke.

Bella thought Mrs. Berkey was grasping for a reasonable explanation. Or she might be right. Bella hoped so. She felt uneasy about the secretary not showing up on time.

"I hate to disturb her," Jax began, "but I want to wrap up all the staff interviews this evening, if possible."

Mrs. Berkey nodded. "Dina's suite is near mine. I can go get her."

"Thank you, ma'am. I'd appreciate that."

As soon as the older woman was gone, Bella laid her pencil down. "What do you think?"

A grin curved Jax's lips. "I was about to ask you the same thing."

Bella beamed in return. The look on his face reminded her of the boy he'd been, and warm memories surfaced. "You go first."

He shrugged. "I hope Mrs. Ryerson is napping. If she's gone, that's not good."

"I feel the same way. What about Miss Lansing's comments?" Bella asked.

"She seemed reluctant to discuss Mr. Anderson. I felt like I had to drag information out of her. Even then, I don't know that she was completely honest. In addition, when I spoke with her before, she didn't say anything about taking cars to Anderson. Overall, she seemed protective of him."

Bella bit her lip. "I noticed. But, if she and Anderson have some sort of relationship, that could explain her hesitance to say too much."

Jax's green gaze widened in what appeared to be amazement. "You really think the two of them are courting or such?"

A low laugh escaped Bella. "It isn't impossible, you know. People, even middle-aged people, fall in love and, the way Mrs. Berkey spoke about Anderson spending time in the library...well, it made me wonder why people gossiped about him and Miss Lansing." His expression grew even more incredulous as color rose in his cheeks. Bella watched in fascination. Had the mention of love disturbed him so greatly? Or was the tryst between the older couple bothering him?

"That's true. But what does it mean in terms of Anderson possibly being a suspect and Lansing trying to protect him? If they had a relationship, but Anderson showed interest in Crabtree, that would be a motive for the librarian to do away with her friend, but not for him. So, why would she want to protect him from being interviewed?" Jax asked.

Bella gathered her thoughts and scanned her notes before responding to the question. "She might want to keep their relationship secret. After all, he could've lost his job because of their friendship, or whatever it is. As far as I know, Miss Lansing isn't as wealthy as Miss Crabtree, so her job is probably important to her. Maybe she's worried about being fired for fraternizing with another employee on school time."

Jax pushed an errant lock of blonde hair off his forehead. "You may be right, but Anderson has been gone for a couple of years at least, so he isn't an Boxmore Hill employee."

"He might still come around. Mrs. Berkey doesn't seem to know, but others might. I hadn't thought to ask Ida, or anyone else. Now, I wonder."

"I'll see what Mrs. Berkey says when she gets back. We may find out more if we can speak with Anderson. I hope that will be tomorrow." He studied her face for a moment. "Can you come along and take notes? You've done enough by helping with interviews today. I'd like Nolen to type up all of your work. But having you take notes again tomorrow would help since Nolen will still be out searching." Jax slumped back in the chair in a gesture of weariness. "I spoke with him and Richard earlier, and they both think we need to keep looking for Miss Crabtree. Between Boxwood and here, and along the riverbank from east of Boxwood toward Lake Erie, if we can manage it. We definitely can't send people too far, since we don't have enough help. Nolen is calling all the boys who fought in France. Some have helped already. Richard is contacting constables in a wider area. That would give us enough people to make a better search."

"That's a sound plan, and I'd be happy to help in any way I can." Bella rolled her pencil back and forth across the table. "One other thing I noticed when you questioned Miss Lansing was her referring to Miss Crabtree in the past tense. That seems strange because almost everyone else talks as if she is simply missing."

Jax's gaze clouded. "I noticed that, too, and it's troubling."

Bella glanced at her notepad. "Also, Miss Lansing first said Miss Crabtree was often late, like it was expected. Later, she insisted her friend would be in a hurry to return to school as a reason for her not going to Anderson's place."

For several moments, Jax studied Bella's face. "Good catch, because it's odd, and I didn't note her saying it. Miss Lansing evidently wants us to stay away from Anderson, which is also strange. You could be right about her not wanting their relationship to come out, though. It's hard to say what her motivation might be."

"Anderson's place isn't on the way here from Boxwood. It's a few miles to the northeast. If Miss Crabtree went there, her entire route would form a triangle with the longest side being from the Anderson home to Boxmore Hill."

"With no straight lines involved. Parts of all those roads run along the river or creeks. Some go through dense woods," Jax pointed out.

"You've probably traveled more of that area than I have. I've been on the main highway, but the directions from Miss Lansing make it look like Anderson lives in an out-of-the-way place."

"He definitely does from her little map and from what she told us, too."

"I still think it's strange that Miss Crabtree headed out there on Friday night," Bella said. "If she needed repairs, she might have to leave the vehicle. If so, why not ask Hilliard to follow her? It had to be getting dark when she left his farm."

"Like we already discussed, she might have wanted him to go along until they argued," Jax said.

"But she went anyhow."

"Maybe. Maybe not. We still don't know for sure."

"But we know Miss Crabtree has rarely been in a rush to get back on time, let alone early. She only did this time to please Mr. Hilliard."

"Who remains a suspect, in my mind." He laid his fingers flat on the table. "Another unusual thing was Miss Lansing knowing so many details about Anderson's plans. Of course, that could be explained by your theory about them courting."

Bella was about to speak again when Mrs. Berkey, her face pale and drawn, returned. "Dina isn't in her suite. I asked several of our teachers if they've seen her. One did shortly after dinner, but evidently, Dina never returned to her rooms."

Both Bella and Jax stared at her. "Where else would she go?" he asked.

The headmistress swallowed convulsively. "Miss Dobbs saw Dina walking down the path leading to the library and chapel, but both are closed after dinner. The parking area is in the same direction. I didn't walk out there because I wanted to let you know I didn't find Dina."

"None of the teachers had any idea of where she might have gone?" Bella asked, her own concern surfacing in her voice. Could Mrs. Ryerson's absence be coincidental? Or did it relate to Miss Crabtree's disappearance?

"No, I spoke with several whose rooms are near her suite. Dina hasn't been seen there since this morning. She left the office to go to dinner, but planned to be back before her meeting with you." Concern was evident in her tone and expression. "She is very reliable and responsible. I can't imagine her not being here for the interview." Mrs. Berkey wrung her hands.

"Does she like to walk the grounds?" Jax inquired.

The headmistress shook her head. "Not really. Dina enjoys tennis, but not walking or hiking. I've never known her to do either one, especially in the evening."

Jax's jaw tightened. "There's a bit of daylight left, so I'll cover the campus. Before that, I want to call my deputy and let him know we might have another missing person. He can come over in case we don't find her shortly." Jax looked at Bella. "Would you get a few teachers and search the other buildings?"

"Of course," she agreed, "but there are very few places to go. As you know, the offices, dining room, theater, and gymnasium are in this building. The classroom building is locked at four o'clock. The library and chapel are in separate buildings, but, as Mrs. Berkey said, both would be secured at this hour."

Jax looked back at the headmistress. "Does Mrs. Ryerson have keys to the various buildings?"

Mrs. Berkey nodded. "We have a set here. Let me see if they're missing." She returned only moments later with a key ring in her hand. "None is gone."

"I'll check the grounds, but I need to know if her vehicle is here," Jax told the headmistress.

"I'll look now," Mrs. Berkey told Jax. "It's an old black Packard. None of the other teachers have similar vehicles."

"I'll go, and you can wait in case calls come in," Jax replied. Briefly, he turned to Bella. "Let's meet back here in thirty minutes. Nolen should arrive by then. If necessary, he and I can head off-campus to look for Mrs. Ryerson. It's late to get a search party together, but we could call a few of the other veterans to help us out. We'll see what we find here first."

Bella felt uneasiness spread through her. Two people were missing under suspicious circum- stances. Was there only a kidnapper at work, or was there a killer? The questions made her stomach knot. "I hope that won't be necessary."

"So do I." As Bella started out of the room, Jax caught her sleeve. "Don't search for Mrs. Ryerson alone and don't let anyone else do that, either. We don't know what, or who, we're dealing with and I don't want teachers or students taking chances."

The intensity in his gaze telegraphed genuine concern. "We'll all be careful," she assured him, "but you take care, too." The words reminded Bella of their earlier exchange, as well as Ida's observations. If Mrs. Ryerson and Miss Styles were behind Miss Crabtree's disappearance, had they joined up to escape? If so, they might not be out of the area. The same could be true if they'd partnered with Hilliard. And what about Mr. Anderson? Were he and Miss Lansing involved? Or was he guilty, and she was only trying to protect him? Caution was needed until they knew a lot more.

Some indefinable emotion flickered in his green eyes. Then, he nodded. "I will." Jax dropped his hold on her and followed the headmistress to use the telephone.

Warmth from his light grasp lingered, but Bella focused on the case and turned toward the main hall.

Chapter Nine

A FTER TALKING WITH NOLEN, Jax went to the dining hall. He tried opening the double doors,
but they were locked. From there, he headed outside. The student and faculty dormitories had lights
glowing from the windows. Since searching those
buildings was already being handled, he walked
down the brick path to the library. Gas post lights
provided illumination as the sun disappeared. But
would a lone woman come out this way at dusk?
With its remote location, the campus undoubtedly
seemed safe, so maybe.

Before continuing to the far end of the parking
area, Jax stopped at his Chummy to retrieve a flashlight. The beam wasn't strong, but it would help.

He glanced around as he walked. In the distance,
the library stood as a shadow. Certain that Mrs.
Ryerson wouldn't have gone to a locked building,
he continued through the parking area. Once there,

he searched for her old Packard but didn't see it. By the time Jax got to the back edge of the area, sunset had fallen, so he pointed the flashlight at the ground. Just as he was about to return to the office, he noticed a glint in the deep grass. Jax moved closer and stooped down to get a better view. The reflection was from a pair of broken spectacles. He moved closer to study them more carefully. Had they fallen out of someone's bag or pocket?

Anxiety rippled along his spine as Jax searched his memory for an image of Dina Ryerson. He hadn't seen her wearing spectacles, but perhaps she only needed them for reading. Or maybe they belonged to someone else and weren't a clue at all. Unsure of their importance, Jax pulled a handkerchief out of his pocket and carefully picked them up. If they were evidence, they needed to be treated with care.

As Jax headed back to the main building, he continued to scan the ground. His heart beat faster, but he tried to quell the hope churning along with it. He badly wanted an excellent piece of evidence, but he knew better than to count on this being the one.

Bella was trying to calm a nervous Mrs. Berkey when Jax walked into the office. Mrs. Berkey, obviously agitated, was trembling. "This isn't like Dina at all," she said, repeating her earlier assertion.

"I know," Bella said before turning to Jax. "Several groups of teachers searched the student and faculty dormitories. None of us found any trace of Dina. What about you? I don't suppose her car was still here."

"No, it's not," Jax replied, "but I found these in the deep grass at the far end of the parking area." He pulled a handkerchief out of his pocket and unwound it to reveal broken spectacles. "Do they look familiar to you, Mrs. Berkey?"

The headmistress stepped forward. For several moments, she studied the glasses. "Why, yes, they do. Miss Crabtree has a pair exactly like them. Two other teachers wear similar ones, but they've been wearing them every day. Of course, someone might have just lost them." Her voice trembled as badly as her hands.

"If you'll give me their names, I'll ask and see," Jax said.

"Of course." The headmistress jotted down two names and handed a slip of paper to him. "You can use the telephone on Dina's desk. The operator will connect you to the faculty dormitory. That will be faster than you walking over there."

Jax thanked her and made the call. Getting both teachers on the line took a few minutes, but he soon had answers. After hanging up, he said, "You were right, ma'am. Both of them have their spectacles. You're sure Miss Crabtree is the only other one on campus with ones like these,"

The older woman, her face ashen, met Jax's gaze. "Yes, constable. Very sure."

Both uneasiness and hope hit Bella. Did they finally have solid evidence? "Did Miss Crabtree always wear them? Or were they only for reading?"

"She was never without her spectacles," Mrs. Berkey replied. Her voice was still tremulous.

"So, she wouldn't have lost them before leaving on vacation?" Jax asked.

"Definitely not. She wouldn't have been able to see to drive." The ringing of the telephone interrupted. "I don't know who would call at this hour." Mrs. Berkey disappeared into her office.

Bella turned to Jax. "If those belong to Miss Crabtree, and she needs them, how did they get to the other side of the parking area?"

"That's a good question," Jax replied. "I thought they might be Mrs. Ryerson's, which would have made more sense."

"Clues don't always seem sensible right away."

"That's true." Jax put two fingers to his temple and rubbed. "Someone could have inadvertently dropped them. A parent bringing a child to school, for example. Or, someone might have planted them."

"Planted them. You mean to make us think someone from Boxmore Hill is involved in Miss Crabtree's disappearance?" Mr. Hilliard came to mind since he'd been on campus earlier in the day but hadn't told them.

Jax nodded. "I need to do more checking to make sure Mrs. Berkey is right about these belonging to Miss Crabtree, but that seems likely. If we go on that assumption, there are the two possibilities I mentioned, as well as a third. At this point, I think it's unlikely that a stranger is involved, so the guilty party might have been on campus and inadvertently dropped them.

"I agree." Bella leaned against the secretary's desk and folded her arms over her waist. "Three of the five suspects have been on campus today: Mr. Hilliard, Mrs. Ryerson, and Miss Lansing."

"You're including the former groundskeeper when you say five."

"We know little about him, but yes. Aren't you?" Bella asked.

"I am, but we don't know how long the spectacles were there. The grass is long at the end of the parking area, and there's no walkway."

"Which means the perpetrator didn't have to be on campus today. Or whoever dropped them, since we can't be sure they belong to Miss Crabtree." She clasped and unclasped her hands. "We can ask Mrs. Berkey if students or teachers go out there often. I haven't seen anyone do that myself, but I haven't been around for long."

"Good idea. I still want to put finding Mrs. Ryerson as a top priority tonight. Even though she's a suspect, she could be a victim instead."

Mrs. Berkey returned as Jax was speaking. "Another concerned parent." She wrung her hands. "I heard you say you want to look for Dina yet tonight."

"My deputy should be here any time. When I spoke with Nolen, I asked him to stop at the Boxwood dry goods store on his way here, just in case Mrs. Ryerson went to see Miss Styles. Does she have other friends in the area? Or another place where she might go?"

The headmistress shook her head. "Although Dina was a student here, she and her husband lived in New York for years. When she was hired for the secretarial position, she indicated she'd be on campus almost all the time since her only friends and acquaintances were in the city, and she was estranged from her family." Her brow furrowed. "Occasionally, she takes a drive, but doing so now...I can't believe she would. With Miss Crabtree missing, I'm very concerned. What do you think, constable?"

"I'm not sure what to think," he reluctantly admitted, "but we need to spread out the search for her. Perhaps, she went to see Miss Styles." The idea provided no solace. If the women were together in Boxwood, Nolen would have located them by now and called the school. Evidently, he hadn't, which increased Jax's anxiety. What, if anything, did the spectacles mean? Surely, they were a clue. "In any case, he'll watch for a disabled vehicle on the roadside. After I speak with him here, I'll drive the other roads in the immediate area myself. The darkness presents a challenge but, if she doesn't get back tonight, we'll start searching again after dawn. At that time, we'll have more area veterans, and some constables from nearby towns."

"Thank you, constable. Perhaps some of my teachers could also help again. Even tonight, we could go in several vehicles," Mrs. Berkey suggested.

"I appreciate the offer, but I'd rather you didn't, ma'am. For now, I think it's best if you, your staff, and students stay on campus, especially overnight."

"All right," the headmistress said.

"Mrs. Berkey, we wondered if many people walk out beyond the parking area where Jax found the spectacles," Bella said.

"No, not as a rule."

"I see." Bella sighed.

"May I use your telephone again? I'd like to get Richard Jenkins to help us out this evening. He's staying at my house during the investigation, so he's not far away."

"Certainly," the headmistress replied before leading him to her office.

Once Jax spoke with the senior constable, he turned to Bella. "Do you mind walking me to my car?"

"Of course not." She glanced at Mrs. Berkey. "Is there anything else I can do?"

The headmistress shook her head. "I'll stay in my office until later, so I'm here if anyone calls, but there's really nothing for you to do right now, Miss Stewart. Go ahead to your room and get some rest. You've had a busy day and evening."

Jax focused on the headmistress. "I'll call you by eleven o'clock, Mrs. Berkey, and let you know what we've found, if anything, and see if you have any news. As you said, Mrs. Ryerson may have taken a drive and planned to be back long before dark. If she simply wanted some time to herself, we don't want to alarm people or cause her embarrassment." He paused for a moment. "If she took a drive, her car may have broken down. If so, we're likely to find her on the roadside." He hoped that would be the case.

The woman nodded, but her expression remained grim.

Jax held the door for Bella and walked beside her as they headed down the corridor toward the exit. Once they reached the parking area, he turned to her. "What are your thoughts about Mrs. Ryerson now?"

When she faced him, Bella looked as apprehensive as he felt. "Running off seems like a sign of guilt, but maybe I'm borrowing trouble. As Mrs. Berkey said, she could have taken a drive. Possibly to Boxwood to see Miss Styles. It would save a lot of worry and trouble, if she's there."

"As I said, I asked Nolen to call me if he found her. Since he didn't telephone, I think we can rule that out." He absently massaged his right bicep as he spoke. "Richard is going to drive out by the Anderson place, and see if he's home. He's getting a fellow constable from up the road to meet him there, just in case."

"That's smart," Bella agreed.

"After finding the spectacles, I want to be cautious. It's doubtful Miss Styles was here in the past few days, since she has no vehicle. But we know Grover Hilliard, Mrs. Ryerson, and Miss Lansing were. We also know Anderson is very familiar with the campus. With Miss Crabtree supposedly heading his way late Friday, and Miss Lansing referring to her in the past tense, I'd like to know something more solid about the man. So far, he doesn't have an obvious motive to kidnap or kill Miss Crabtree."

"But Dina Ryerson does." Bella put a hand to her forehead.

"So do Miss Styles and Hilliard." Jax paused. "It's really frustrating not to narrow the suspects down to only a couple by now."

"We didn't in the last case. At least until the very end."

Jax offered a slight smile. "You're right."

"And you were right that a missing person case is more of a challenge than a homicide."

A rueful grin played across his lips. "Being right doesn't make me feel any better about our lack of progress."

"Finding the spectacles could be key. I noticed you handled them carefully. Fingerprints could help."

"I'll see about getting them printed," Jax said, "but we need something as a match. Getting prints from various people will take more time."

"Mrs. Ryerson and Miss Lansing live on campus, so their rooms would have their fingerprints, wouldn't they?"

"There will be prints." Jax massaged his temple again. "We won't get results for days, and it's been a week since Miss Crabtree disappeared."

"But you haven't been working the case very long. Only a few days," Bella said.

His amusement drained away. "Which is a long time when a woman has disappeared. And now, a second one is gone."

Bella released a long, low breath. "It's extremely disturbing, I agree. Are you still planning to talk with Mr. Anderson in the morning or will Richard interview him tonight?"

"Richard will ask some questions, if the man is home. Afterwards, he'll head over here and help us search. I'll call Mrs. Berkey later." Briefly, he studied Bella's face. "For tonight, stay inside and advise other teachers to do the same. I won't be back this evening unless we find Mrs. Ryerson, but I'll come first thing in the morning. Please don't do any investigating on your own, or with Ida, before then. I don't know exactly what's going on here. Like I said, a stranger probably isn't responsible, but—no matter what—I don't want to take chances."

Bella nodded. "We won't go anyplace tonight, and I'll be here in the morning."

Jax smiled. "Good. We can talk tomorrow about interviewing Anderson. For now, that's on the back burner."

Headlights briefly hit them before a vehicle pulled up and stopped. Nolen leaned out of the driver's side. "The school secretary wasn't in Box-wood, but neither was Miss Styles."

Briefly, Jax let his head fall forward. "Does anyone know where Miss Styles is?"

"I tracked down Mrs. Kendall, who said Miss Styles got a ride to Moreley from the town photographer and took the six o'clock train to Columbus," the deputy replied.

"Did he leave, too?" Bella asked.

"No, he drove her is all. She got a call about a teaching position and went for an interview." Nolen looked at Jax. "Mrs. Kendall said Miss Styles was in a big hurry."

"Did Miss Styles mention the name of the school to her employer?" Jax asked.

Nolen shook his head. "I asked, and she didn't."

"Mrs. Ryerson was at dinner when other teachers were talking about the case and how Miss Crabtree might have disappeared. A couple wondered if someone kidnapped her, which led to a discussion of who disliked her," Bella said.

"I'm guessing Mrs. Ryerson and Miss Styles were mentioned."

Bella nodded. "They were, and Mrs. Ryerson had to overhear, since she left pretty soon afterward."

"I didn't hear the conversation at your end of the table," Jax said. "No one near me discussed possible suspects."

"You sat by Mrs. Berkey, and she would have curtailed such talk, I'm sure."

"Probably," Jax replied before mulling over Bella's revelations. "Mrs. Ryerson left at least fifteen minutes before we did, and Mrs. Berkey thought she was very quiet. Since she was at the opposite end of the table, the behavior must have stood out to her." It hadn't to Jax, but he'd been thinking about Ida's warning and watching Bella. He had to focus on the investigation.

"Mrs. Ryerson said little, and Mrs. Berkey knows her well enough to notice unusual behavior. What bothers me now is that she had time to call and alert Miss Styles about the speculation at dinner," Bella said to Jax.

While he listened, Jax shifted from one foot to the other. "That's true. With both Miss Styles and Mrs. Ryerson gone, I'd like to know if they talked this evening. I'll go back to the office to contact the local operator before leaving here." He turned his attention to Nolen again. "Richard is on his way, but he'll go to the Anderson place first. Were you able to get any volunteers to drive some of the side roads?"

"About a half-dozen are coming. I meted out general areas," Nolen replied. "And I said what you told me about only spending a couple of hours searching this evening."

"Good. Even with headlamps and flashlights, seeing very far in the dark will be darn difficult. I'll run back to the school office and make that call. What area is left for me to search?"

After his deputy answered, Jax returned to the building and Nolen went on his way. Bella fell into step next to Jax. Neither spoke on the way to the office, and she waited patiently while he talked to the operator. When he put the earpiece back on the candlestick, Jax sighed.

"You heard my end," he said.

Bella nodded. "Dina Ryerson called Miss Styles around four o'clock."

"Yep, and it definitely puts the two of them in the spotlight. Not to mention that Mrs. Ryerson was most likely in the parking area this evening."

"And Hilliard, since he took Miss Styles to Moreley and was on campus earlier today."

"Right, so I need to see if he's home. I'll call him now."

That connection took longer, but the operator finally got Hilliard on the line. Jax asked a few questions about when the photographer had last spoken to Styles and Ryerson, and about taking the former teacher to the Moreley train station. He also inquired why the man hadn't mentioned being at Boxmore Hill that morning.

As soon as the call ended, Bella began asking questions. "Did he know more about where Miss Styles has gone? What did he say about not revealing his trip over here?"

Jax put up one hand. "Whoa. First, she didn't tell him the name of the school, either, and she had a large carpetbag with her. He thought that was odd because it's supposed to be an overnight trip. As for being here, he didn't think it was important, but he hesitated long enough to make me suspicious about a cover-up."

Bella was as suspicious as Jax, but she had another question. "You asked him about Mr. Anderson, too. What did he say?"

"Hilliard insists he knew nothing about the man working on cars or about why he left his job here. Years ago, he met Anderson but only in passing. He could be lying to me." He drove his fingers through his hair. "There are so many bits and pieces of information to take apart and put back together. Not to mention the spectacles, which may or may not be important."

"I know," Bella agreed.

Jax leaned against the doorjamb. "I need to get going. I'll ask Mrs. Berkey to talk with you after I call. That way, you'll know what I know."

"Good. Otherwise, I'd wonder and worry."

For a moment, Jax's gaze met hers. Finally, he simply said, "Have a good night, Bella," before straightening up and turning away.

"Jax..."

He glanced back over his shoulder.

"Be careful."

Some emotion flickered in his green gaze before fading away. "Always." Then, he was gone.

The reply did little to quell her anxiety. He and Matt had both said they would be careful in France, but her brother was dead and Jax had been badly wounded twice. As she headed toward the teachers' residence hall, Bella found her fear growing. Ryerson and Styles could be in cahoots. If so, they would probably have left the area. On the other hand, Styles could be on her way to a job interview and Dina might have simply taken a drive. What if both she and Miss Crabtree had been kidnapped and killed? What if the person was waiting to strike again? Most importantly, who was responsible?

When Bella returned to her room, she found Ida waiting anxiously. "Were there any breaks in the case? Did you get any interesting details from anyone? Or did Jax say you couldn't share information with me?"

Bella laughed at her friend's quick questions. Undoubtedly, Ida had been waiting with them in mind. "There was nothing confidential." She briefly summarized the main points from the interviews before revealing Mrs. Ryerson's unexplained departure.

Ida frowned. "Mrs. Berkey is right. That is completely unlike Dina. At least from what I know of her. She goes for drives, but not at night. Her car is an old junker."

Fresh anxiety filled Bella. "I hate to think of her stuck on the roadside after dark, but that seems like the best possibility." Better than her being involved in Miss Crabtree's disappearance.

"It does," Ida agreed. "Maybe she wanted to get away for a bit."

"That's a possibility. Jax looked around out there while we were searching in the dormitories and saw no sign of her."

"I wish I could have helped, but I was tutoring several students. I was dying to ask what was happening when you stopped by the study room, but I was afraid the girls would carry tales, if I did."

"Good thinking," Bella replied. "The biggest news is Jax found a pair of spectacles, and Mrs. Berkey is sure they belong to Miss Crabtree."

Ida's hand flew to her mouth. "Mrs. Berkey would recognize them, and I've never seen Miss Crabtree without them. Where were they?"

"At the far end of the parking area in deep grass."

"Hardly anyone goes out there."

"That's what Mrs. Berkey said, which isn't helpful. They could have been dumped or lost days ago."

"Dumped?"

Bella nodded. "Jax thinks they might have been planted there to put a focus on someone from school. I thought about it walking back here. Since Mr. Hilliard was here this morning, he could have placed them there."

"Since that area isn't heavily traveled, how would that help?"

"He might not know that, but Mrs. Ryerson would. Still, it doesn't seem like a good place to hide the spectacles." Bella scratched her head. "A lot remains perplexing."

"I agree with you."

Bella thought back to the day's interviews and shared important bits. "From what we know, Miss Styles and Mrs. Ryerson regularly commiserated about Miss Crabtree's treatment of them. We knew she got Miss Styles fired, and evidently, she planned to call board members after Easter vacation, so Mrs. Ryerson would also be dismissed."

Dismay blanketed Ida's face. "Did Dina know?"

"Mrs. Berkey told her and urged Dina to get along as best she could but, perhaps, it was too late." The idea seemed quite possible.

Ida nodded her head. "It's no secret that Miss Crabtree belittled Dina's choice of husband when they were in school and now. That had to be painful for Dina. I know I'd be upset if someone berated me about Alan. It would add to the grief."

"I'm sure it would." Bella forced her thoughts away from her friend's sorrow and to the case. "Miss Crabtree was the one who caused most of their problems."

"Absolutely." Ida grimaced. "Even worse, Loretta Crabtree lords her wealth and status over Dina."

No wonder there were bad feelings between the two women, but were they bad enough for Mrs. Ryerson to lash out? Much of the evidence pointed in that direction. But a lot pointed elsewhere. "What happened to Mr. Ryerson was sad," Bella agreed. "I can understand why his wife holds a grudge toward

Miss Crabtree and why she didn't hurry to do tasks for her. It doesn't seem like Mrs. Ryerson would want to come back after what happened. Not when she knew Miss Crabtree was still around."

"Remember, Dina was in a desperate situation. Mr. Ryerson left here without a reference, so they had to live on what he made from odd jobs, private lessons, and selling his own work. Unfortunately, working other jobs didn't give him a lot of time to paint." Sadness darkened her hazel gaze. "Maybe I should have said so already, but I've heard they were deeply in debt by the time he died. A gallery owner who showed Mr. Ryerson's paintings loaned them money, but it had to be paid back."

"Didn't Mrs. Ryerson ask her parents for help? Surely, they didn't still believe Mr. Ryerson was a fortune hunter after years had passed."

"They were both dead by the time he became ill, and they left their entire estate to various charities. The rest of her family ignored her, too." Ida shook her head in dismay. "Dina needed a job and a place to live. Here, she has both, so she doesn't have a lot of expenses."

Bella's heart constricted. "She's had a very hard time, but I wonder why she continuously antagonizes Miss Crabtree. I'd think she'd keep a low profile and avoid any issues."

"Dina is sweet, but she dug in her heels when dealing with Miss Crabtree. Or so it seems."

Ida's opinion gave Bella pause. She mentally reviewed the interviews again. Mrs. Berkey had also indicated Dina stubbornly refused to kowtow to Miss Crabtree, and Miss Styles had given similar indications. If Dina was headstrong, was she also volatile? That would give credence to her being involved in Miss Crabtree's disappearance. Bella's pulse raced with fear. What would Dina do if the lawmen caught up with her? "Do you think she would harm anyone?"

A look of surprise crossed Ida's face. "Dina? I wouldn't think so."

"I hope not." But hope was rather insubstantial. Apprehension was not.

"I can't imagine Dina and Miss Styles doing away with someone. Of course, I don't know Miss Styles. Dina may be stubborn with Miss Crabtree, but that doesn't make her dangerous. If I had thought it was even remotely possible, I would have told you and Jax right away."

Some of Bella's anxiety ebbed. "I know you would have. It's just that Jax, Nolen, and Jenkins are going out to look for her, along with some others. If Mrs. Ryerson did something to Miss Crabtree, she wouldn't welcome being found by police officers."

Ida's gaze narrowed on Bella. "You're borrowing trouble, Bella. I know you helped Jax with three previous big cases, but Dina isn't a dangerous fugitive. She's most likely a stranded driver, and Miss Styles probably is in Columbus about a job."

"You could be right." Unfortunately, her friend could also be wrong. With effort, Bella went on to the other issues bothering her. "Right now, it's impossible to hone in on one person. Jax and I both found it odd that Miss Lansing referred to Miss Crabtree in the past tense, like she was already gone, and she discouraged Jax from talking to Mr.

Anderson. Said he was gone all weekend, so he wouldn't have been home to work on a car."

Ida folded her hands in her lap. "That's strange on all counts. I suppose it's possible she's telling the truth, and Mr. Hilliard lied about Miss Crabtree taking her car for service."

"Unfortunately, we don't know who's lying and who isn't. Jax is frustrated about not narrowing down the number of suspects, and so am I. It was bad enough when only Miss Crabtree was missing."

"Let's hope Dina took a drive and had car trouble. If so, she may turn up tonight."

Bella nodded, but she still felt uneasy.

"Miss Lansing told you where Anderson lives, though?"

"Yes, but only after a lot of wrangling. It was obvious she didn't want to reveal his location," Bella replied.

"Do you think Miss Crabtree might have gone there, and something happened?"

"But why would Anderson harm her?"

A light rap on the door kept Ida from responding. Bella opened it to see Mrs. Berkey standing in the hall. As she studied the woman's face, Bella found fatigue and fear there. Did that mean something had happened? Something bad?

"Come in, please."

The older woman shook her head. "It's late, and I don't want to disturb you and Miss Byington. I simply wanted to tell you that Constable Hastings called. They found no sign of Dina or her vehicle." She kept her voice hushed, but the quaver in it was obvious.

"I'm sorry they didn't locate her," Bella said.

"I was, too. Having two staff members missing...well, it's quite troubling."

Empathy filled Bella. Mrs. Berkey already had a lot of responsibilities in her role as headmistress, and the past few days had added to her burden. "I'm sure it is, but they may find her in the morning. Jax said they'd go out again, if necessary. He may want some of us here to drive the back roads, too."

Mrs. Berkey's features softened. "You know him well, don't you? He said almost those exact same words."

Warmth invaded Bella's face, but she focused on the case, not Mrs. Berkey's observation or Jax. "Did he say what time they plan to start?"

"He'll be here by seven-thirty. I told him we'll serve breakfast until eight o'clock since we won't have chapel tomorrow. I invited him, his deputy, and the senior constable to join us. He said they would appreciate the hospitality, but he'd like to speak with you about your notes, too. I suggested you use the small room off my office again. He'll look for you in the dining hall when he gets here."

"Thank you, Mrs. Berkey," Bella said.

The older woman nodded. "Good night, ladies."

Bella bid the headmistress the same before softly closing the door.

"We need to get some sleep," Ida said, "especially you."

"I took notes in shorthand, so I need to transcribe everything first. I hope the light won't keep you awake."

"I'm sure it won't," Ida said.

And she was right. In moments, Bella heard her friend's soft snoring. Within an hour, she sought her own bed, but rest was a long time in coming.

Chapter Ten

A S SOON AS SHE saw Jax on Friday morning, Bella knew he had slept no better than she had. In fact, he looked like he might not have slept at all.

"You look exhausted," she observed once he had settled at the table in the small room off the office.

"At the risk of sounding ungallant, you look a little tired yourself." A slight smile played across his lips before his expression grew serious. "I hope you didn't stay up late transcribing notes."

"That didn't take long, but Ida and I talked for a while. She said Dina is stubborn where Miss Crabtree is concerned, but she can't believe Dina would harm anyone. She likes her a lot, as do the other teachers. She's regarded as very sweet and kind, as I told you. Now, I wonder if that clouds their perceptions."

"She might be what she seems. Maybe there's a logical explanation for her disappearance, but I certainly didn't expect another Boxmore Hill employee to come up missing. None of us did." Jax braced his elbows on the table and leaned forward. "Nolen, Jenkins, and I spoke briefly after we got back to the station last night. Mrs. Ryerson vanishing adds a major complication. So does Miss Styles' sudden departure. Dina Ryerson could still be stranded on a side road, especially if there was an accident and she was injured. We weren't able to get to every lane and by-way. Our priority today is to check each road we didn't already access. Some are so rough that trying to drive them at night was tough. Not to mention, visibility isn't good on those side roads and headlamps only do so much."

"True. Dina might have thought she should stay with the car, if there was an accident or breakdown. After all, navigating the roads in the dark wouldn't be easy for her, either. Maybe she'll walk for help this morning and Miss Styles may be back from Columbus soon."

"Both are possible," he agreed, although his voice held no note of confidence.

"Mrs. Berkey said the teachers will help search. About half have vehicles."

He nodded. "Jenkins is speaking with her right now. We have a plan, and he's sharing it. Part is asking for help with driving the back roads. We don't have enough manpower to do it efficiently, so a few more searchers will be great. As it is, everyone Nolen and Richard recruited will help us search for Mrs. Ryerson this morning." Jax ran one hand over his face. "Since we know Mrs. Ryerson left between dinner and her appointment with us, there's a shorter time frame, which means she's apt to be in the immediate area—if she didn't take off."

His final caveat made Bella uneasy. "What about talking to Mr. Anderson?"

"That's still on my agenda, but for this afternoon or early this evening. Finding Mrs. Ryerson is the top priority. Of course, we also want to locate Miss Crabtree."

Her attention focused on his drawn face. "You can't work all day and all night."

Jax looked grim as he met her gaze. "We have two missing women. Time is important, and a week has passed since Miss Crabtree was last seen." Frustration was obvious in his expression and voice.

Bella laid her hand on his forearm. "You can only do so much, Jax."

For a moment, Jax watched Bella before putting his other hand over hers. The warmth in his grass green eyes was also in his voice. "Thanks, Bella. Sometimes, I need to be reminded of that." A smile pulled up one corner of his mouth.

His light touch affected Bella far more than she cared to admit. Far more than it would if he was actually her brother. Dismay flickered through her. How would she react if it was Matt making such a comment? She kept the idea in mind as she spoke again. "I'll remember that."

Jax grinned as he moved his hand away. "I'm sure you will."

"We don't have time to go over my transcription now, but I'll drive your car and you could read it. I don't know if much applies to Mrs. Ryerson's disappearance, though." Bella moved her hand from his arm to the table, but she was still very aware of him. She hoped he didn't realize it. The confidence Bella felt in Ida's reassurances quickly slipped away when she was close to Jax.

"That's a good idea. I called about getting finger-prints from the spectacles. It will take a few days, mostly because someone is going to pick them up from my office. I said we were too shorthanded for me to send a person with them. If they get good prints, we'll go from there."

"That's progress," Bella said with a smile.

"A little." He glanced at his pocket watch. "If we want to eat, we should probably get to the dining hall. In less than an hour, it will be light enough to search."

Only a handful of students was at breakfast when they arrived, but the faculty table was filled. Much to Bella's relief, Ida had saved two seats next to her at the end. Bella let Jax take the one next to Mrs. Berkey and across from Jenkins while she settled beside her friend. This was the perfect position to avoid excess conversation with the teachers, es-pecially Eliza Dobbs, who was apt to ask a lot of unwanted questions. And flirt with Jax.

"We've set up teams already," the senior constable told them once they sat down. "We have ten vehi-cles, so we should be able to cover all the side roads by one o'clock. The teachers will go out in groups of two or three. If they see anything unusual, they will come back to the school. Nolen will wait here to talk with anyone who returns early, maybe with news."

After a long swallow of coffee, Jax replied. "That will work well." Then, he looked at the head-mistress. "I hope we haven't taken too many of your teachers. You'll need some here to supervise students."

The older woman looked grim. "Few of our students are still on campus. A number of parents have either picked up their daughters or plan to do so today," Mrs. Berkey said. "By tomorrow morning, all the girls will be gone."

"Please make sure the girls don't wander off until then," Jax advised in a troubled tone. "We don't know who or what we're dealing with, so extreme caution is best."

"Constable Hastings is right," Jenkins agreed. "Keep the girls and the teachers together as much as possible. I assume both the faculty and student dormitories are locked."

Mrs. Berkey nodded. "The doors are always secured at night, but I advised our custodian and our groundskeeper to keep them locked until further notice. The teachers all have a key to their building, but the girls will have to come to the office if they want access to their rooms during the day. The few remaining will be in the faculty living room with two teachers who won't go on the search. Between six and seven this evening, our housemother will be in the dormitory's lobby to let them in following dinner. They'll need to stay inside until morning. By tonight, I doubt if we'll have more than a half-dozen girls still here anyhow."

Jax glanced at Richard. "I think we should consider security at both residence buildings overnight, if we don't solve these disappearances by then."

The older man rubbed his chin as if in thought. "You're already very shorthanded," he pointed out.

Mrs. Berkey interceded. "We have several empty rooms in the teachers' residence. We'll get them ready. Then, the remaining girls could stay there tonight. I'm sure the staff would take shifts at the front desk. Our janitor and groundskeeper would probably help, as well. There is a parlor near the front door with two sofas, so they can sleep there. We have gas lights outside, so they're always on. Do you think that would provide enough protection?" She looked from Jax to Richard and back.

Jax was about to volunteer to spend the night himself when Jenkins spoke. "I think it's an excellent suggestion, ma'am. Keeping the doors secured will go a long way to making the building safe." He looked at Jax. "What do you think, constable?"

"It should be fine," he agreed. After all, if the senior constable thought it was a viable strategy, why should he find fault with it? Besides, Bella's observation that he took too much on himself was still in the back of his mind, as was her advice that he couldn't go completely without sleep. "Mrs. Berkey, please impress upon your teachers and students that, until we solve the disappearances, everyone needs to remain cautious."

"I'll certainly do that," the headmistress agreed.

Finally, only the lawmen and Bella remained at the table. Richard Jenkins leaned back in his chair and folded his arms across his chest. "We have a bit of time before the sun is completely up, and we can set out. Since this is the first that we've all been together to talk in detail, I'd like to hear what the rest of you have to report. Nolen?"

"I've mostly driven around looking for Miss Crabtree and then, Mrs. Ryerson, but I've looked at Bella's notes." The deputy gave her a quick grin. "And I spoke with Mrs. Kendall at the Boxwood dry goods store. You all know about Miss Styles going to Columbus for a teaching job."

"It's late in the school year to be hired," Richard pointed out.

"Mrs. Kendall said a teacher eloped over Easter," Nolen said, "so they need someone right away."

"That makes sense," the senior constable replied. "Anything else of importance?"

Nolen shook his head. "Unfortunately, no."

Richard looked at Jax. "You think it's suspicious that both Miss Styles and Mrs. Ryerson left after speaking on the telephone?" When Jax nodded, he continued. "Added to their dislike of Miss Crabtree and you finding the broken spectacles, I agree about them being strong suspects. Maybe the strongest." He glanced around the table. "I suppose we all do." After Bella and Nolen nodded, he continued. "According to the notes, Miss Lansing acted oddly during her interview. Any additional thoughts about her?"

"Bella and I both found it strange when she referred to Miss Crabtree in the past tense. Then, I had to drag Anderson's location out of her, and her entire attitude seemed odd. She acted upset about her friend being missing. She dabbed at her eyes, but they were dry." Jax tapped his fingers on the table. "A lot points to Styles and Ryerson, but I can't shake the impression that Lansing is hiding something."

"As I've said in the past, gut feelings should never be ignored. They can help us solve cases, and you have a lawman's instincts, Jax. We can keep her at the top of our list," Richard said.

The senior constable's compliments brought color into Jax's face, which evoked conflicting emotions in Bella. He was a good constable, and he was getting better. She wanted Jax to be happy in his new life but hated thinking he'd put the past completely behind him. Sometimes, it seemed like he put the wonderful memories, so vital to her, behind him, too.

"Another thing bothering me is how Mrs. Berkey acted when she talked about Anderson leaving. She hemmed and hawed around, not wanting to explain what the campus gossip was," Jax said.

When he stopped talking and looked at her, Bella offered more information. "Evidently, some of the older teachers think he was fired because of spending an undue amount of time in the library. Mrs. Berkey didn't want to go into details, but speculation is that he and Miss Lansing were smitten with each other. Perhaps, they still are."

"Really," Richard murmured. "That would explain why she takes her auto to him, and why she might have convinced Miss Crabtree to go there, too. But I wonder why she didn't share his whereabouts with other teachers. If he only got a small inheritance, extra money would come in handy. Besides, when I drove out there last night, there were several vehicles in the yard."

"Money is often a motive for murder, isn't it?" Bella asked in a thoughtful tone.

"It is," Richard said. "Why do you ask?"

"Dina Ryerson took the job here because her husband left her with no money. When Jax and I spoke with Miss Styles, it was clear she's struggling financially, as well." Bella paused. "I've been thinking about that, and it makes sense as a motive in this case, but how would they get money from Miss Crabtree by kidnapping her?" Her assertions sounded weak, even to her own ears.

"Miss Crabtree was very wealthy. She liked to shop and spend money, so she must have taken cash with her on trips," Jax pointed out.

"You brought up a good point, Arabella, and you have an excellent insight, Jax." Richard braced his elbows on the table and folded his hands in front of him. "Another notion comes to mind. If Crabtree took her auto for service, she would likely pay in cash. Anderson would certainly know about her carrying a lot of money. If he got fired and his inheritance was small, he might have a monetary motive.

If Miss Lansing is sweet on him, she could've helped him."

"Good points," Jax agreed. "I could talk to him this morning instead of later today."

The senior constable shook his head. "One constable from over Anderson's way is going to drive by his place this morning. I told him not to confront the man alone, but he'll know if Anderson is back. I've called some constables on the route from here to Columbus, and they're on the lookout for an old Packard. Even though Styles took the train, she didn't necessarily go all the way to Columbus. She could've gotten off some place and joined Ryerson. That's if she's involved. I also gave them descriptions of the two women. They'll call both the school and your office if anything turns up. It's good you finally have a clerk to answer the telephone."

"Thanks, Richard," Jax said. "You're always a big help."

"I'm only helping. The heaviest load, as usual, is falling on you and Nolen." He shot a smile at Bella. "And your very able amateur associate."

Warmth spread through her at the praise, but it failed to melt the chill of apprehension. Although suspects and clues were plentiful, an answer was yet to emerge. Loretta Crabtree's fate remained a puzzle. Now, Dina Ryerson fell into the same category.

The group quickly reviewed other aspects of the case.

"Hilliard is still a possibility," Richard said. "But he'd need help to get rid of Crabtree's car."

"That's the main thing bothering me about him," Jax agreed. "It's also troubling that he failed to tell

Bella and me about being at Boxmore Hill yesterday. He made a weak excuse about it not being important."

Bella chewed on her lower lip. "The spectacles trouble me. Mr. Hilliard wouldn't necessarily realize that the far edge of the parking area isn't frequented by faculty or students. Mr. Anderson, Miss Lansing, Miss Styles, and Mrs. Ryerson would. In fact, faculty and staff park back there."

"Miss Styles doesn't have a vehicle," Nolen said.

"So, she didn't leave the spectacles, intentionally or unintentionally, but any of the others might have," Bella put in.

Richard glanced at the windows. "Since it's nearly full daylight, we need to meet with the searchers. What we discover, or don't find, this morning could be key."

The group headed outside where volunteers—veterans, local lawmen, and teachers—waited. Jax gave a few instructions and wrapped up by saying everyone needed to be back at the school by one o'clock. With that, people dispersed.

Chapter Eleven

A FTER DRIVING THEIR DESIGNATED section and finding nothing, Jax said, "This may be a fool's errand. I can't imagine an old car making it through some of these bad sections. I'm not even sure Mrs. Ryerson came this way, since she and Miss Styles could have planned a getaway."

"But we had to search for her. As you said, she may be a victim, not a suspect."

Jax pulled out his pocket watch. "We better head back or we won't be there by one o'clock when everyone is supposed to return. I hope some of them were more successful than we were."

"I do, too, but since heavy rain started, seeing any distance is difficult."

"It is, but you're doing an excellent job of driving. Like always."

His compliment stood in contrast to Griff Biggins' hesitancy to ride with Bella, which pleased her. She and Jax might be going in different directions since the war, but they had a lifelong connection that hadn't been completely severed. "Thanks. It's more fun to drive the Chummy in pleasant weather," Bella said as she peered into the slashing precipitation.

"I agree. Putting the top down is a treat. Of course, we're getting plenty of fresh air anyhow." Jax injected a note of amusement into his voice.

"Along with some water, which is why I can't go too fast. With no side curtains or Isinglass, we'd be soaked."

"There's no rush," Jax said. "Everyone else is dealing with the same issues."

"True." Bella continued back along the route they'd taken. Heavy clouds joined with the rain to make visibility poor, especially when they got to a section where trees stood sentry on each side. Anyone with claustrophobia would have been ill-at-ease. As it was, a feeling of dread swathed Bella. The chilly dampness didn't help. A hot meal and warm room sounded like heaven. Another forty minutes, and they could enjoy both.

As Bella navigated a curve, she gasped. An automobile was blocking the road. She quickly downshifted and braked hard to avoid a collision.

"That was close," Jax said. "Good job on stopping."

"Too close for comfort," she murmured, looking at the vehicle only ten feet away. Her heart raced, and her breath came in quick gasps. "I wonder why it's in the middle of the road. The driver should have pushed it off to the side, and I don't see anyone in it." Was the person unconscious on the automobile's floor? Walking for help in this weather would have been a last resort.

Jax had no chance to answer because a male voice interfered. "Turn off the car and take your hands off the steering wheel, Miss Stewart."

Apprehension and dread tangled inside Jax as he glanced out to see a gun pointed into the vehicle from his side. The man's face wasn't familiar. He looked at Bella, who was sitting stock-still.

"Now." The word, hard and harsh, was an order.

"Do as he says," Jax told Bella. Meanwhile, he struggled to organize his thoughts.

As soon as Bella followed the instructions, her door was flung open, and a handgun appeared next to the driver's side window. "Toss your gun out, constable," a female voice ordered from Bella's side of the car.

"Both Fanny and I are armed." The man moved closer, put his hand through the window, and pressed his pistol against Jax's temple.

Fresh frustration hit Jax like a freight train. His service revolver was in his jacket pocket, but he couldn't get it out and fire before one of them got a shot off. If a bullet hit Bella...his mind shied away from finishing the thought. What other choices did he have?

"Throw your weapons away, Hastings," the woman barked. "And don't try any heroics. If you do, Miss Stewart will be the one who suffers, and if she tries anything, Andy will take care of you."

"I only have one gun," Jax replied, while silently cursing himself. Lansing and Anderson, who was obviously the one holding a weapon on Jax, were in cahoots. Now, her insistence that the man had been away made perfect sense, since she clearly hadn't wanted Anderson questioned. Or he'd been getting rid of Loretta Crabtree and her vehicle before needing to do the same with Dina Ryerson. Jax inhaled deeply to regain his focus. Bitter aggravation formed a knot in his gut as he withdrew his gun and tossed it out the window. Protecting Bella was his primary concern. But how? Unarmed, he had few options. "You won't get away with this. Many people know where we're searching. When we don't get back to campus, Deputy Rogers and Senior Constable Jenkins will realize something is wrong. You won't elude them for long."

"Don't be so sure, Hastings," the other man said. "Get out of the car slowly and turn your back to me. Keep in mind Miss Stewart will be in Miss Lansing's gun sight the entire time. Pull anything, and she's a dead woman."

Jax ground his teeth until a muscle jumped in his jaw, but he withheld comment. Instead, he eased out of the car. When he didn't immediately turn away from Anderson, the librarian barked another order.

"Don't try anything foolish. Just do as you were told and do it quickly." The woman waved her weapon as she spoke.

Immediately, Jax stood still. "You're making a big mistake. You can't possibly get away with this."

Fanny Lansing laughed. "I think we will. Andy and I have two hostages, and I don't believe your deputy or that retired constable will try to take us when we have guns on both you and Miss Stewart. That's if we encounter them, which is unlikely. By the time they realize the two of you are missing, we'll be far from here."

Jax's mind whirled with the effort to come up with an idea to get Bella out of harm's way. Only one strategy came to him, so he said, "Let Miss Stewart go. One hostage is enough, and a lawman is the best kind of hostage. No one will try to arrest you while I'm along."

"Oh, constable," the librarian said with a shake of her head. "That's very noble of you, but I'm sure you'll be easier to control if we have your friend along. And I'm sure she'll behave with you under the gun." She turned to her accomplice. "Andy, tie Hastings up."

The former groundskeeper—of medium height but stocky build—pulled a rope out of his pocket and moved toward Jax. "Turn around and put your hands behind your back."

Jax ground his teeth, but presented his wrists. When Anderson grabbed his arms and forced them back even farther, Jax bit back a groan. His bad shoulder didn't like the abuse, but that was the least of his worries. Lansing and Anderson had probably killed already, so there was little to stop them from doing so again. That knowledge turned his stomach. He glanced at Bella, who was still in the Chummy.

Her eyes were wide with alarm. Was she thinking about last spring when she'd been kidnapped? He and Mac had saved her then. Now, rescue seemed unlikely.

Anderson tied Jax's wrists tightly. Rain continued to fall, but at a slower rate. Jax glanced around. Could he somehow take out both Lansing and Anderson? Unlikely since she was out of his reach.

"Now, you get out, Miss Stewart and step around to the front of the car. Remember, if you try anything, Constable Hastings is a dead man," Anderson said.

The sneer on Anderson's face made him look like a fierce predator, not the unassuming, agreeable groundskeeper that people had said he was. What caused the change? Or was he great at hiding his true demeanor? Not that it mattered. Jax hadn't given up on him as a suspect, but he hadn't expected an ambush, either.

"Andy, push the constable's car to the side of the road. I'll keep the two of them in my sights. I'm sure neither will make a wrong move."

Once Anderson did as Lansing told him, he was back with his own gun pointed at Jax's head.

"Get in the driver's seat, Miss Stewart." Lansing looked at Jax. "Constable, you get in the back seat on the driver's side. Andy will sit with you, and I'll be in front with Miss Stewart. I advise both of you to do exactly as you're told. Otherwise, one of you will suffer."

"You go first, constable," Anderson said. "And remember, my gun is on you, and Miss Lansing's weapon is on the lady."

Jax needed no reminders.

Bella did as bid, and Jax followed instructions, as well. Finally, all four were in the vehicle.

"Don't drive too fast or too slow," the former groundskeeper said from the back seat. "And don't try something funny. Do you understand me?"

"Yes," Bella murmured over the lump of fear and dread choking her. Few viable solutions existed when they were at the mercy of two killers, both holding guns. With no alternative, Bella steered the car down the road.

For an indeterminable time, miles passed without seeing a house coming into view. Eventually, they'd go by a farm, but would someone be outside? It was highly unlikely Lansing and Anderson would choose a route through or near a town. Even if Bella saw someone, how would she attract attention without risking Jax's life and her own? Their situation seemed hopeless.

Jax had said the lawmen would eventually catch Lansing and Anderson, but when? She and Jax weren't expected at Boxmore Hill for another half-hour. In that time, they could end up in Lake Erie or someplace else equally final. Although Bella was unable to see either Jax or Anderson, except as shadows, the groundskeeper probably wouldn't stop aiming his pistol at Jax. Unsure if the man would act on his threat, Bella tried talking to them.

Distracting the pair seemed like her only choice. If she did, Jax would have a chance to act. Surely, he'd think of something. After all, he'd saved her last spring when she'd been kidnapped by a killer. "You did a good job of framing Mrs. Ryerson," she began, "and Miss Styles."

A cackle-like laugh left Lansing. "Both made their dislike of Loretta obvious all along. That was a big help to us, and it made them look guilty. The two of them meeting for dinner Friday was a bonus, and Dina being out alone last evening played into our hands."

"What about Miss Styles? Senior Constable Jenkins and Deputy Rogers will talk to her," Bella said. With luck, their abductors wouldn't know Miss Styles was out of town. The groundskeeper's reply ended that hope.

"She called Miss Lansing about a reference for the teaching job in Columbus. By the time she gets back from there, we'll be gone," Anderson said. "Even if we weren't, Bertha isn't aware that we kidnapped Loretta or Dina."

"Where are they?" Bella asked, wondering if she really wanted to know.

A moment of hesitation preceded the librarian's response. "Dina is in Andy's house. She's safe but trussed up, so she won't be going anyplace. Loretta is permanently away, shall we say?"

Although the statement didn't shock Bella, it created additional anxiety. "I thought you and Miss Crabtree were close friends," Bella said.

"She thought so, too." Lansing laughed.

The librarian's cutting tone, heartless assertions, and dark amusement made Bella cringe. Poor Miss Crabtree. As mean as she'd been to Dina and Jeffery Ryerson, she had made a terrible mistake in choosing Lansing as a friend.

"But why would you kill her?" Bella asked, still confused.

"Her parents had an extensive collection of jewels and coins," Lansing replied, "She used to keep them in her room, but I finally persuaded her they'd be better off in the library's safe."

"The library has a safe?" Bella asked in surprise.

"We have some rare books. They're usually in a locked case by the circulation desk. However, when school is closed, I store them in the safe," Miss Lansing replied. "For the past couple of years, Loretta has put her valuables in my care. This year, Andy and I decided we'd waited long enough. We want to enjoy the money before we get too old."

Clearly, the pair had been plotting for years, which only increased Bella's horror. How diabolical. "You'll have to sell everything to get money. That will cause suspicion to fall on you."

Lansing guffawed. "You must think me very foolish, my dear. We'll get money from Andy's cousins, and they'll sell some items in Toledo and Cleveland as reimbursement. We can sell off the rest bit-by-bit, not enough in one place to arouse interest." The librarian leaned back in the seat. "I don't imagine anyone in Europe will ask a lot of questions. We already have passports, in assumed names, of course."

"What will you do when you've sold everything? How will you live then?" Bella asked, mostly to keep the woman talking. Perhaps, getting their captors to discuss their plans could distract them.

"There's more than enough to keep us going for many years," Anderson said. "And live in style while we do. Loretta's parents left her a lot of money. For years, she's flaunted her wealth and taken advantage of her position. If not for her interference, Jeffery would have had a successful career as an artist instead of ruining his life, his spirit, and his health by doing back-breaking physical labor. I just wish he was alive to enjoy some of her money. We roomed together years back. Shared the old caretaker's cottage on the campus. I had to quit school after the fifth grade. Could barely read or write, and Jeffery taught me both. It was a terrible day when he got fired, and all because of Loretta."

The depth of Anderson's loyalty to the former art teacher surprised Bella, which explained a lot. "Are you sharing the funds with Dina?" Bella asked. If so, why had they left her tied up?

"No, my dear," the librarian said. "Dina has no stomach for our plans, and Jeffery probably wouldn't have, either."

Sudden understanding came to Bella. "She had no idea that the two of you killed Miss Crabtree until she was abducted herself last night. If you had told her what you planned to do, she would have turned the two of you in."

A sigh left the librarian. "She probably would have. Last night, she was getting something out of her Packard when Andy and I were outside talking.

Unfortunately, she overheard the two of us, which meant we had to kidnap her."

"We didn't harm her," Anderson said. "I couldn't do that. But, as Fanny told you, Dina is tied up in my house. Down in the root cellar. The trap door is under a dresser. I imagine someone will find her in the next day or so. Now that the two of you are missing, your friends will do a thorough search. She'll be all right until then."

Bella realized why none of the lawmen who visited Anderson's place had seen anything out of order. But why hadn't they noticed Dina Ryerson's Packard? "Where have you been all this week, and where are the cars?"

"I been in and out," Anderson replied. "I met my cousins last weekend when I took Loretta's car to the lake and pushed it in. I brought Fanny back before then, so she wasn't missed. My cousins were a big help, since they lived along the lakeshore all their lives, and the two of them make runs up and back from Canada from time-to-time."

"They're rumrunners." Jax's words were a firm statement.

Jax sounded calm, but Bella felt her apprehension escalate. Since Prohibition started in 1920, the illegal alcohol business had increased with every passing month. Because the trade was lucrative, more and more gangsters were getting involved. With their participation came violence. If Anderson's relatives were bootleggers, they probably didn't shy away from bloodshed. Evidently, they'd assisted Anderson in disposing of Miss Crabtree. Chills rippled through Bella, but she tried again to keep

Lansing and Anderson engaged. "What about Dina Ryerson's car?"

"It's in Andy's cousin's barn," Miss Lansing replied. "He'll dump it in the lake as soon as he can. Dina never saw the cousins, so she won't implicate them. Getting rid of the car will ensure they're never questioned."

"The cars will be found eventually," Bella said, although she wasn't sure that was true. Even if they were, it would likely be far too late for her and Jax.

"We'll be gone by then, and my cousins won't be tied to us or the vehicles," Anderson said.

"What about the spectacles?" Jax asked. "One of you must have planted them, but they didn't point all suspicion away from you two. We all discussed it this morning, so Nolen and Richard know about them."

"It was an oversight that they didn't go into the lake with her," Anderson said.

"Yes, it was," Miss Lansing agreed in a tart tone, indicating disapproval. "They must have been in Andy's vehicle. When he dropped me off at the very edge of the parking area, I retrieved my cloak from the trunk. The spectacles evidently fell out then. I was in a rush since I needed to return to my suite before someone missed me."

Bella didn't need to be told that Miss Crabtree had been transported in the trunk. Another shiver rippled through her. "Since you both have weapons, I assume one of you shot your friend."

The librarian's wicked humor returned. "I did. She never knew what hit her. It was that quick.

Everything went exactly as we planned, except for the lost spectacles."

"We suspected you for a while," Bella said.

"I know. But you also considered Hilliard, Bertha, and Dina." Lansing shifted to look back at Jax. "After we caught Dina eavesdropping, I told Andy we needed to take her Packard, so you might focus on her and Miss Styles. As it is, Dina vanishing means that evidence will point her way a while longer. Once they find her, she'll identify us, but we'll be long gone."

"The spectacles probably have your fingerprints," Bella said, "and they're going to be tested." But that would take time. Probably too much time.

Again, the old woman released a humorless snicker. "My dear, I'm a librarian. I do a great deal of research, and I'm aware of fingerprinting. You need prints to match. It will take even longer to retrieve those, if you can get clear ones. I imagine we'll be halfway across the Atlantic by then."

Bella's insides knotted, so she returned to her earlier argument. "Your plan to get out of the country quickly may not work. We're expected at school." Jax had tried the same explanation, but Bella didn't know what else to say.

"I heard the plans to meet on campus by one o'clock," Lansing said. "No one will worry immediately. Even if they head straight to Andy's house from Boxmore Hill, which is unlikely, the drive will take them over thirty minutes. Once they find Dina, they'll talk with her. Of course, they have no notion of where we're going, and they won't be able to call other cops from his place since there's no phone.

By the time they get organized, we'll be partway across Lake Erie."

"You're going to cross the lake right away?" Jax asked. "That seems foolhardy."

Anderson chimed in. "The sooner we get away, the better. My cousins expect us since I drove up there with Dina's auto. One brought me back, and he'll have his boat ready by now. We'll head to Pelee Island right away. Few people on the island now, so we can make a clean getaway. No one will connect me with the cousins because we have different last names, and I've never mentioned them to anyone at Boxmore. Of course, no one cares about the former groundskeeper. The students are snobs, and so are most of the teachers. Crabtree was the worst of the worst."

The pure hatred in his tone made Bella shiver. So did his revelations. The pair had a plan, a diabolical and deadly plan, one that they'd put in place long ago.

"She certainly was," Lansing said with another chortle.

Anderson laughed, too. "I heard the two of you solved three major cases last year, and I expected more of a challenge."

Several seconds of silence preceded Jax's response. "Yep, we solved those cases together," he replied in a tone devoid of emotion. "They were quite interesting. The one in August had an unusual situation to begin with, and the one last April had an interesting climax. Car accidents were involved in both."

Accidents. The word echoed endlessly in Bella's head. Was Jax suggesting she make one wild attempt at freedom by crashing the automobile? His careful wording made that seem likely. But where? Simply running off the road wasn't apt to help.

Bella watched the passing scenery closely. Overcast skies made gloom an impediment, but she knew this section well since she'd been on it hundreds of times. Several farmhouses sat close to the road. Although they weren't grouped together, she only needed help from one place. The rain had changed to a steady drizzle, so someone might be out doing chores. Besides, bad weather didn't keep farmers inside. If she saw anyone, Bella could veer into the ditch and hit the horn at the same time. *If* was the important word. What if no one was out?

After passing two houses and seeing no sign of activity, sweat moistened her palms and her mouth went dry. If she didn't act soon, they would move into less familiar territory and closer to their ultimate destination. As she contemplated forcing a crash, Bella wondered again if Anderson would shoot Jax immediately. With few alternatives, she decided to run off the road at the next homestead. As soon as a house came into view, she inhaled deeply, slowed down, and swerved toward the ditch. At the same time, she banged the horn repeatedly.

To Bella, the honking sound seemed to come from faraway. Her entire focus was on maintaining control of the car as it ran off the road and tilted sideways before coming to a thumping stop in the ditch. For fleeting seconds, relief spread through her. Miss Lansing had been thrown against the dashboard where she laid still and quiet and harmless.

Bella grabbed her door handle and scrambled out of the vehicle. Maintaining her balance on the side of the ditch wasn't easy, but she got enough traction to grab the outside handle on Jax's door. As she did, a gunshot cut through the silence. When a low moan followed, Bella felt bile rise in her throat. Anderson must have shot Jax. Tremors ran through her as she struggled to stay on her feet.

The next few moments passed in a blur. Two men ran out of the farmhouse. As they got closer, Bella realized she was at the Fox homestead and yelled, "It's Bella Stewart. Constable Hastings is with me, but he's been shot. We were kidnapped. The people who did it are here, too." The words came out in a staccato rhythm, but she wanted their rescuers to have details quickly and fully. How she expressed so many details, Bella would never know.

"Where are these crooks, Arabella?" Mr. Fox's voice cut through the air, along with the sound of two shotguns being cocked.

"Both are on the right side of the car, so they can't get out of there," she replied. "The one in front is probably unconscious, but the one in back is armed and awake." At least, Anderson had been conscious moments earlier. "Please help me get Jax out." Her voice was plaintive as panic filled her. Anderson had gotten off one shot. Had the bullet, as promised, gone into Jax? Was he already dead? Had she done the wrong thing by running off the road?

The questions swirled through her mind without finding answers while shivers racked her body.

Suddenly, Mrs. Fox was by Bella's side. "Let me help you, dear."

"Go inside with my missus. Hettie, get the operator to call the constable's office and see if Nolen is there. If not, call his house," Mr. Fox called to his wife. "Edwin and I will see to Constable Hastings."

"Nolen should be at Boxmore Hill," Bella said.

"I'll try both places and Doc Smedlay, too." Mrs. Fox grasped Bella's arm. "Come with me. The rain has let up, but you're soaked and need to get warm and dry."

"What about Jax?" Bella saw both Lansing and Anderson were lying quietly inside the car. Evidently, he had got off the shot before losing consciousness himself. Or the gun had gone off in a reflex action. She looked toward Jax and detected movement. Perhaps, he wasn't badly wounded after all.

Edwin Fox's soft voice was soon in her ear. "It looks like your captors are out of commission. Pa and I will see they stay that way."

"Let me look at Jax," Mr. Fox said. When he climbed out of the ditch, he focused on Bella. "I don't think it's too bad, so we can carry him into the house, but I don't want to leave those other two alone."

Bella wanted to believe the older man, but she hovered nearby. Anxiety still filled her. Jax was now motionless and silent. Not good. Not good at all.

Chapter Twelve

THE NEXT THIRTY MINUTES passed quickly. Mrs. Fox ushered Bella into the house and made the calls. Afterward, she wrapped a blanket around Bella and handed her a cup of tea. Within moments, the Fox men carried Jax in and laid him on the couch. In the lantern light, his face looked pasty white, but it was the sticky moisture covering his left jacket sleeve causing the most concern for Bella, who still trembled with anxiety. Relief filled her when Doc arrived. As soon as the physician prodded at the wound, Jax's eyes fluttered open.

"Just lay quietly and let me look at you," Doc said.

"It's not bad," Jax muttered, but it sounded as if his teeth were clenched.

Bella laid the teacup aside and perched on the edge of her chair. At least Jax was talking. That had to be a positive sign.

After a moment, Doc concurred. "You're right. It's a flesh wound, but you've bled a lot. Let me get it cleaned and bandaged."

Within a short time, Jax's arm was bound, and he was sitting up. To Bella's eyes, he looked pale and shaky. "Shouldn't you lie back down?" she asked.

"I'm okay." Jax avoided her gaze.

"You will be, if you don't push yourself," Doc commented. "The bullet took a chunk of flesh when it grazed you. I'll leave some antiseptic powder. Make sure you check the wound tonight and put some of it on. I want to make sure you don't get an infection. You don't need any additional issues with this arm when your right shoulder and bicep still give you trouble." With that, the older man nodded to Bella and walked out with Mrs. Fox.

Bella tossed back her blanket. "How did you get hit in the left arm? Anderson was on your right."

His gaze moved to her, but it seemed slightly unfocused. "As soon as you veered toward the ditch, I threw myself at him. I hoped to knock the gun loose, but at least he hit his head in the tussle."

"Miss Lansing did, too." As she studied his pale face and bandaged arm, Bella felt another stab of guilt. "When you mentioned the auto accidents, I thought you wanted me to cause one."

"I did." Jax studied her for a long moment. "You shouldn't feel guilty."

Tears pricked her eyes, and she blinked hastily to keep them at bay. "You got shot."

"The bullet grazed me, nothing more. If you hadn't crashed the car, we'd be in Lake Erie within the next hour and not for a swim. You did the right thing, Bella. The only thing that could have saved us."

"I suppose so."

Mrs. Fox returned with her husband and son. The older man focused on Jax. "You're looking better, constable."

"I am better, too. What about Anderson and Lansing?" Jax asked.

"Deputy Rogers and Senior Constable Jenkins are here and have them shackled. They plan to take the pair to your jail," Mr. Fox replied.

Jax levered himself to his feet.

When he wobbled slightly, Bella got up and rushed to his side. "Take it easy."

"I will," he assured her, "but I want to talk with Richard and Nolen before they leave. They need to get to Mrs. Ryerson as soon as possible."

Bella's concern for Dina had taken a backseat over the past hour. As Jax went outside, she followed close behind.

While the three lawmen talked, Bella listened carefully and hoped Dina was safe, as Lansing and Anderson had said.

After Nolen and Richard left, Jax turned back to Bella. "I'm going to ask Mr. Fox to take me to my Chummy. Then, I'll head over and talk with Mrs. Berkey. You can come along, if you like."

"Fine, and I'll drive." She certainly didn't want him driving himself. She didn't even want him sitting up. As far as Bella was concerned, he should be resting. Since that was unlikely, she was going along.

They said little on the trip to get the Chummy. Once in it and on their way to the school, Bella periodically shot sidelong glances at Jax. When his eyes closed, she wasn't sure whether to feel relieved or worried. He needed sleep, but what if he lapsed into unconsciousness? Bella fought the repeated urge to ask if he was all right.

When they arrived on campus, she parked in front of the door to the main building. After Jax woke up and said nothing about putting the vehicle in the lot, she figured he wasn't as fine as he'd said. With that in mind, she stayed close to his side all the way down the corridor and into the headmistress' domain. Mrs. Berkey started in surprise when she saw the bandage on Jax's left arm.

"What happened?" she asked, looking from Jax to Bella.

Bella revealed the news to the headmistress, who immediately told Jax to sit down.

"I'm all right," he said.

"You look white as the driven snow," Mrs. Berkey replied. "Now, sit down before you fall down. I'll fix you a cup of tea. That may help warm you up. Your clothes are damp, but we have nothing for a man." Her attention went to Bella. "You should change into something dry, Miss Stewart."

Although her first inclination was to protest, Bella didn't have a chance to speak.

"I'll stay with the constable and make sure he's comfortable," Mrs. Berkey said.

The woman was being both kind and bossy, but Bella didn't mind. Not when the woman would look out for Jax. "All right," Bella agreed before hurrying off.

Once in Ida's room, she quickly changed clothes, gave Ida the latest news, and returned to the office. She found Jax in the same chair and Mrs. Berkey in one next to him. The headmistress had most likely mothered many students. That she wanted to do the same for Jax touched Bella deeply. For a moment, she studied his face. His color was better.

"Are you ready to go home?" she asked him.

"I'll head to the office first," Jax said. He got to his feet before speaking again. "Thank you for the hot tea. I'll be in touch when I know more about Mrs. Ryerson."

"Thank you for telling me your deputy and the senior constable went to get her. I won't rest easy until I hear she's safe and sound," Mrs. Berkey said.

"I'll contact you with details later today," Jax said.

After both Bella and Jax bid goodbye to the head-mistress, they headed into the main hallway.

"I can drive you back to Moreley," Bella said. Her worry about him hadn't ceased.

For several moments, he gazed down at her. The concern on her face made his heart thump errat-ically. They needed time alone, time for him to finally reveal the truth about her brother's death.

But the car wasn't the best place. After he divulged everything, she might want to escape his presence. He glanced away and swallowed hard. "Let's find a quiet place to talk."

Seconds of silence ensued before she spoke. "Why don't we talk in the Chummy while we're on our way?"

"There must be some spot on campus. The sun is out, and it's warmer."

Her gaze ran over him. "I have dry clothes, but you're damp around the edges and wet in places. Not to mention, you're wounded."

"It's really nothing," he assured her. "You heard Doc say it's a flesh wound." If Jax didn't talk to Bella soon, he feared losing his nerve—something he'd done too often for too long. Using his current condition as an excuse wasn't a good idea. "Let's find a private spot here."

"All right," she agreed, although her expression was puzzled. "There's a little gazebo in front of this building. It's off to the side and secluded. No one will be there now." Bella led the way in silence.

Once they settled on the bench, Jax took a long, reassuring breath. "There's something I need to tell you, something I should have told you two-and-a-half years ago. Something that's kept me running hot-and-cold, as you've noted more than once."

Confusion clouded her gaze and furrowed her brow. "Two-and-a-half years ago would have been during the war."

He leaned forward, braced his elbows on his knees, and put his head in his hands. "It was."

Several seconds of silence ensued. "Is it about the French nurse?"

The completely unexpected question made him sit up straight and look at her. "French nurse," he echoed. "What French nurse?"

"The one who was with you the day after Matt died."

With one hand, Jax massaged his forehead. He hadn't given the woman, Celeste, any thought in this context. All of his concentration was on how to reveal the truth without causing Bella more pain. Or making matters between them worse. "No, not about her." Another extended period of stillness increased his discomfort, and it escalated when she spoke again.

"Are you sure? I mean, I've wondered if she was someone special to you." Bella folded her hands in her lap and stared down at them. "You didn't introduce us."

Realization hit Jax as her words and tone registered. "Did you think I was smitten with her?" Was that possible? He'd never considered the idea.

Bella looked back at him. "Of course."

"Oh, Bella." Now, he needed to reveal another deeply hidden secret. "I wasn't. Not ever," he began before hesitating. For a while, he'd debated about breaking his promise to Alan Brewster. Should he now?

"Who was she?"

As Jax met her gaze, he realized revealing everything was necessary. This was getting him off-track, but he couldn't let Bella's mistaken belief endure. "Alan met her when her brother, a French soldier, was wounded and taken to an American field hospital. Celeste came looking for him and stayed on after he died. Matt and I got to know her, too, but only in passing. When Alan was wounded, she took care of him, so they got much better acquainted."

"That was kind."

"I suppose so."

"You suppose so. Wasn't she a good nurse?" Bella asked.

"She was an excellent nurse and a kind person. She was the one who told me Matt died when I was still in the field hospital myself."

Slowly, Bella nodded. "Which is why you were together, but I don't understand why you didn't introduce us."

If he'd had any idea Bella thought he'd been involved with Celeste, Jax would have broken his pledge long before now. "I promised Alan that I wouldn't say anything about her. Both Matt and I did."

"That makes no sense."

Of course, it didn't and it wouldn't until she knew the entire story. "The short version of a long story is Celeste and Alan fell in love, but he didn't want Ida to know."

Shock slackened Bella's jaw as she stared at him. "Alan fell in love with another woman." Astonishment echoed in her voice.

Jax wasn't sure if it was a question or a statement, but he answered. "I'm not sure it was love, but he thought so. I'd say it was more like infatuation with both of them. They spent every free moment together for weeks until Alan died."

"Now, I realize why he didn't see Ida when he got away from the line. He was with the nurse."

Bella was obviously, rightfully, upset on her friend's behalf. "I'm afraid so. Matt and I both tried to convince him he was being foolish, but it did no good. It's hard to say what he would have done. He didn't seem sure himself. I only know Alan swore us to secrecy."

"Maybe he planned to come home and marry Ida after betraying her. That would have been as bad as marrying someone else. I can hardly believe Alan did something so awful."

"I was in complete disbelief. Matt and I didn't want to hurt her, so we agreed to keep quiet."

A pause preceded her next statement. "You could have told me, especially after so much time has passed. Why didn't you?"

"I felt bound by the promise, Bella, and I figured you'd be upset. I wasn't sure if you'd keep it from Ida or not."

Shock and dismay widened her gaze. "I'd never do or say anything to hurt her," she said, her voice firm with resolve. "You should've realized that. She's my best friend. Like a sister."

"I know you wouldn't hurt her, and I probably should have told you before now, but I didn't think you'd taken much note of Celeste."

She sighed. "When the two of you walked away together, I was hurt. I wanted to cry on your shoulder over Matt's death."

After a moment, he leaned back and closed his eyes, but that day in France was vivid in his mind. And he felt as guilty now as he had then. Guilty and ashamed. "I should have cried with you, but I could hardly face you." He glanced back at her.

Once again, she looked puzzled. "Why would you have guilt about Alan's actions?"

"I don't," he replied. The moment between those two words and his next sentence stretched long and wide and deep. Finally, Jax revealed the crux of the dilemma. "My remorse is about Matt's death."

The confusion in her dark gaze slowly became speculative. "Are you talking about when you left Paris that weekend, and you promised to keep my brother safe? That wasn't possible, Jax. You were often at a distance from one another and, even if you hadn't been, you had your duties and he had his. You couldn't have protected him. I realized that."

Revealing everything was every bit as difficult as he'd feared, and maybe worse. But going back was impossible. "I should have told you the whole truth long before now. First, facing you that day in France was awful. Then, after losing your parents, too, I didn't want to add to your pain." He ran a hand over his face. "Finally, I couldn't stand having you hate me."

"Hate you? That would never happen, Jax."

Her sable brown eyes held a wealth of emotion—warmth, concern, admiration, and maybe more. Unless he was very lucky, they'd all disappear when she heard the whole story. He shook his head. "You say that now, but you don't know what happened, Bella."

"Then, please tell me."

The soft entreaty in her voice reached deep inside him. So many times, Jax had considered how to explain. Now, he went back to the simplest part. "You've accused me of running hot-and-cold with you since Matt died. And I have."

"You said you couldn't bear to speak about his death that day in France, and I understood. Not then, but when you finally explained last summer. Now, I realize you were covering up for Alan, too."

Her soft sympathy was appealing. Not that he deserved it. "You don't know why I couldn't talk about it. I've barely been able to face you since Matt fell." He swallowed convulsively. "When we work together on cases, I let down my guard, and it almost feels like things between us are the same as before the war. To when everything seemed possible. To when we might've been more than childhood friends. Then, I realize going back to our old relationship isn't feasible and moving forward might not be, either. And that's all on me."

"I don't understand what you mean," Bella murmured.

Her complete confusion made Jax realize he had to be blunt. Prolonging his explanation would only hurt her more. He inhaled deeply, exhaled completely, and looked away. After another long inhalation, he met her gaze. "I sent your brother to die in my place. It was my fault, Bella, all my fault."

She frowned. "What do you mean? Matt didn't die in your place, Jax. He died. It was terrible, but it isn't your fault. It couldn't be."

For several moments, he remained silent. During that time, an image of her smiling up at Biggins floated in his mind. The golf pro was a lighthearted sort who would never hurt Bella. Jax was sure of that. Biggins was exactly the kind of man who should be in her life. Eventually, he could be a partner in the resort, as Jax could not. When he'd resolved to reveal the truth and throw himself on her mercy, Jax figured they still had a chance. But should he expect one? As a tense silence fell between them, Jax stared into the distance. What was best for Bella?

"Yes, it is," he continued, his voice raw with banked emotion. "You just don't know it. I know, and I should have told you when we crossed paths in France after Matt's death. Facing what I'd done then was almost impossible, and you were already heartbroken. I could see the devastation in your eyes. I didn't want to hurt you more. Or maybe I couldn't face your reaction to the truth." He shook his head. "Maybe that's why I haven't told you in all this time." Although Jax sometimes thought about why he hadn't leveled with Bella, he never reached a firm answer. But today, the answer was clear: he was a coward. Not so much physically as emotionally. And not with everyone, only with Bella.

"I don't understand."

Her puzzled expression wasn't surprising. He hated the need to provide more details. He hated the details. But she deserved to understand. "It was my foolishness that killed your brother. I didn't mean for Matt to die, but I can't say I had no idea that it was a possibility. I shouldn't have let him go. I should have gone. I was supposed to go." Even to his own ears, the explanation was messy and muddled. He took several deep breaths and struggled to order his thoughts as he shifted to face her. "Matt came to see some of his men in the field hospital, and I was there, too. He was going on a two-day leave. He would have seen you. Instead, Matt took my place with my men."

Again, a delay preceded her response. "Why would he take your place?"

"My men and I had been at the front. We were ordered over the top and two were killed. Several were wounded. I caught a bullet. Afterward, most of my platoon was being sent back to the line. Everything was mixed up by then. Units were combined due to the number of casualties and illnesses. On top of the gas, artillery barrages, and German sniper nests, flu was running rampant..."

Her voice cut through his. "That still doesn't explain what you mean by saying Matt took your place."

Jax, unable to hold her gaze, looked at a point over her shoulder. "When he visited me in the field hospital, Matt said I should take a few more days to recuperate. He said someone would take my place with my men, but I didn't want just anyone leading them. I didn't want someone who might put his own glory before their welfare." When Matt had visited him, pain from his physical injuries and emotional turmoil had kept Jax from sleeping, even though he was exhausted and medicated. In retrospect, he knew he hadn't been thinking clearly, but Jax didn't use those excuses with Bella. She deserved the unvarnished truth. "Matt didn't have to try hard to convince me he should go in my place. He was a good friend and an outstanding officer. He always put others ahead of himself. He put me ahead of himself." His hands tightened until his fingernails scored callused palms. "Anyhow, we discussed it and, finally, we talked to the major who approved Matt going back to the line in my place."

For long moments, Bella stared at him in complete silence. Endless time stretched out until the hush became oppressive. Unable to watch consternation darken her lovely face any longer, Jax got to his feet. "Saying I'm sorry is far from enough, and I know it. I've regretted letting him go every day since then. If I could go back, I'd change it all." Jax shoved his hands into his pockets to keep from reaching out to her. "I can drive myself back to Moreley."

Bella, pale with shock, said nothing. When her failure to react became denunciation, Jax turned and hurried back to his Chummy, and drove away.

As Bella watched him go, she battled incredulity. Forming a coherent thought proved impossible and, she simply stared after Jax until he disappeared from view. She reviewed snatches of his comments. *Died in my place. Shouldn't have let him. Talked to the major.* Although she understood the logistics of what had occurred, the details made little sense.

Bella wracked her mind to recall more particulars from what Jax had said. *Talked to the major who approved Matt going in my place.* Because Jax hadn't wanted just anyone with his men, her brother had died? Somehow, it didn't mesh with the Jax that she'd known all her life. Finally, she concluded they needed to talk more. She wanted to completely understand. She *needed* to completely understand. By the time Bella gathered her thoughts and followed him, the Chummy was gone.

Numb, she finally turned toward the faculty dormitory and made her way to Ida's room. When she entered, Bella found her friend sitting on one bed.

"I thought you were driving Jax back to town. With classes now canceled for the rest of the week, you could have gone home for a few days."

Bella collapsed on the other bed. "He took off without me."

"What?" Disbelief underlined the single-word question. "Why would he do that? He has trouble driving with one wounded arm. How can he manage with his left arm hurt, too?"

With a sigh, Bella laid down and stared at the ceiling. Emotional turmoil took a heavy toll, as did confusion. She needed to sort out Jax's admissions, and maybe her friend could help. As briefly as possible, she summarized his explanation of Matt's death, and his role in it. She ended by saying, "I was dumbfounded, and Jax took off before I got my thoughts in order. Not that they are now. I'm still grappling with everything he said."

"That's understandable. It had to come as a shock because I'm flummoxed myself."

Bella rolled to her side and faced her friend. "It did." So had Alan Brewster's betrayal of Ida, but Bella would never reveal that. "I want to talk it over with you and try to sort it all out that way." All her life, she'd found it useful to discuss whatever was bothering her. As a child, she'd done it with her mother and grandmothers. Now, she had her best friend to help. And Bella desperately hoped Ida could help.

"Of course." Ida folded her arms across her waist. When Bella said no more, her friend went on. "One thing standing out to me is why the commanding officer let Matt take Jax's place. If Jax was really fine, would that happen?"

Bella chewed on her lower lip. "I don't know." At the moment, she didn't know a lot, especially how to assess the situation.

"It doesn't seem likely to me. This was after Jax got shot the first time. We talked about it before, and you said that might've been a worse wound than the one right before the armistice. Did you ever ask him about it?"

"He always brushes me off, like it wasn't bad. He's the same way about the shrapnel and about getting shot today. Doc said it was a flesh wound, but there was a lot of blood, and Jax got soaked earlier. I changed my clothes, and he didn't. Still, he insisted he was fine."

"Which is what he always does."

Bella nodded. "When they talked about Jax needing more time to recuperate at the field hospital, Matt said someone would go in his place, but Jax didn't want just anyone leading his men." She took some time to consider the implications of his words. "Some in his platoon were from Moreley. Boys, really. Matt and Jax both worried about them, especially after several died."

"Knowing your brother, he didn't want just any-one leading them, either. Not every officer considered the welfare of his platoon. Some were glory hunters," Ida said.

"You're right, and Jax mentioned that," Bella said with growing certainty. "I wish I'd considered that before Jax took off. I wanted to talk more, but I was speechless for a bit."

"He isn't going far. Just to Moreley." Ida's hazel eyes glittered. "If Mac would send the Model T, you could go home for a few days and see Jax while you're there. You haven't given your transcribed notes to him, have you?"

"Not yet."

"Then, get going. The sooner you talk with him, the less time he'll have to withdraw again."

"That's true." Even so, Bella hesitated. "Why don't you come with me?"

Ida considered the request only briefly. "I'll go to Ballantyne with you, but you need to speak to Jax alone."

"I will," Bella replied. "Afterward, I may want a shoulder to cry on."

"I don't think you'll be crying." A slight smile touched Ida's mouth.

"I hope not, but the way he hurried off, I'm not sure it will matter that I don't blame him. He's harbored guilt for a long time, and I'm sure he took my silence as condemnation."

"Maybe so, but you'll explain how shocked you were and tell him you don't hold him responsible. You don't, do you?"

Bella shook her head. "Of course not. If Matt had thought Jax was fine, he wouldn't have suggested someone take his place. I just didn't have time to put it all together."

"You have now, and that's what matters."

Bella called home immediately, but the two friends took Ida's roadster instead of getting a ride. They'd be coming back at the same time, so it made sense. Even so, they spoke with Mrs. Berkey first, which delayed their departure. Finally, they were settled in Bella's suite at Ballantyne around nine o'clock on Friday evening.

"It's too late to drive into town and talk with Jax," Ida said after they both sat down.

"It is," Bella replied. Not that she was ready to face him. Talking with her friend helped put everything in perspective, but she wasn't sure expressing her forgiveness would make any difference in Jax's perspective on their relationship, such as it was. He'd said his hot-and-cold attitude resulted from guilty feelings. He'd said he felt guilty every day. That was a lot of remorse over a long time period. If so, how would they bridge the gap between them? Did he want to bridge it? "I need to take my transcribed notes, but I can do it in the morning."

"You said the two of you need to talk. You're going to do that, right?"

"I suppose so."

Ida frowned. "You're not second-guessing your-self again, are you? Bella, the two of you need to move forward."

"Jax didn't say anything about the future, and he didn't give a reason for telling me all this now. It could be from a guilty conscience, and he finally unburdened himself. It isn't necessarily about the two of us."

"I don't believe that's the reason. Take the notes tomorrow and explain that you don't blame him for Matt's death. Then, see what he says."

"All right. I will," Bella promised. "I definitely will."

Chapter Thirteen

A PPREHENSION STILL PLAGUED BELLA when she parked the Model T next to Jax's Chummy around ten o'clock on Saturday morning. If Richard and Nolen were in the office, as they probably were, how would she manage a private conversation? Should she ask Jax to go for a cup of coffee or a walk? Somehow, she needed to get him alone. Would he cooperate?

When she went into the station, Bella was surprised to see not only Richard, Nolen, and Jax but also a wiry man with black hair, dark eyes, and a thin mustache. He was speaking to the men, so she waited despite fighting anticipation.

"I'll expect you at the end of next week unless your arm doesn't heal properly, Constable Hastings," the stranger said. He turned to the other two men. "Good to meet you, Deputy. Always good to see you, Richard." As he walked by Bella, he touched his forehead as if in salute. "Miss."

Once the man was gone, Richard greeted her. "Glad you're here, Arabella. We were about to wrap the case with a final discussion. Jax was going to call and see about you coming over from Boxmore. Now, he won't need to."

Curiosity mingled with anxiety. A group meeting to tie up *loose ends*, as Jax called them, was standard after a case. But she wanted to talk to him alone. Although waiting would try her patience, she agreed. "Ida and I are staying at the resort until school reopens, so I was home last night. Since so many of the girls already left, Mrs. Berkey decided to resume classes the middle of next week."

"I see," Richard replied. "Why don't we all sit at the table in Jax's office?"

"Like usual," Nolen added with a grin.

Bella tried to smile back, but her lips seemed as wobbly as her legs. Somehow, she had to regain composure. She wasn't some silly little schoolgirl. She was a grown woman. A modern woman. The reminders did little to help. Bella felt as nervous as she had in her first golf tournament as a youngster—damp palms, queasy stomach, and dry mouth. No. She actually felt edgier because so much more was at stake.

Once they were all assembled, Richard began. "Lansing and Anderson were taken to the county lock-up early this morning."

"That's good. What about Dina Ryerson? Is she all right?" Bella asked.

"Yes. She's with Doc and Mrs. Smedlay for a couple of days. She sprained her ankle during the abduction, but she'll be fine." Richard tapped a stack of papers. "We have a statement from her. She overheard Anderson and Lansing talking when she went to her car for her umbrella, so that was true. She never planned to take a drive. After she heard the two of them discussing their getaway, she tried to run, but they grabbed her. She was really surprised they were involved, said Anderson had been a good friend to her husband. At least, he insisted they not kill her, *her words.*"

"Everyone at Boxmore Hill was surprised," Bella said. "Jax thought Miss Lansing was lying, though." She glanced at him, but his expression didn't change. He looked like he was a thousand miles away.

"She wasn't a top suspect to me, either," Jax said in a flat tone without glancing at Bella. "If she had been, we wouldn't have gotten waylaid by her and Anderson on the road."

"None of us figured on that," Richard said. "They're a cagey couple, and they planned for years to steal Crabtree's money. They also organized their getaway in detail."

"All that time, Miss Lansing pretended to be Miss Crabtree's friend," Bella said, moving her attention from Jax to the two other men. "That makes it worse. That kind of betrayal is terrible." When Jax stiffened beside her, she silently cursed herself but had no time to make amends.

"Only the worst sort of person puts himself or herself before a friend," Jax said.

Again, Jax's voice was cold and hard, but the words hit Bella like ice pellets on a winter's day. He'd taken her comment wrong, but how could she explain in front of the others? She couldn't, so Bella bit her lip and tried to focus on the case. When the meeting ended, she'd speak with Jax in private, no matter how she had to do it. And she'd make sure he listened and understood.

"They wanted her money, which isn't a new motive for murder. I've seen it all too often, and we discussed that earlier," Richard observed, seemingly oblivious to Jax's self-recrimination and Bella's anxiety.

Another issue occurred to Bella. "Is Miss Styles back from Columbus?"

"She came on the early train today," Nolen replied. "Mr. Hilliard picked her up, and I saw the two of them at the café right afterward. He was pretty upset, said he wished he and Miss Crabtree hadn't parted with an argument."

"Never a good idea to part with hard feelings or harsh words," Richard said.

Bella agreed, but would Jax agree to further discussion? The example of Grover Hilliard and Loretta Crabtree was another reason to resolve things between them. With effort, she forced personal matters aside. "Did he say why he didn't tell us about going to Boxmore Hill? I know he made a weak excuse to Jax last evening."

Nolen nodded. "He wanted to talk with Miss Crabtree about their falling out. He didn't know she was missing until Mrs. Ryerson told him. He admitted not saying anything because he was afraid it made him look guilty."

"I see." Bella understood the man's reasoning, although he'd been foolish in trying to hide his activities. "What about Mr. Anderson's cousins? Has anyone spoken with them? It sounded like they were accomplices."

"They were," Nolen said, "and more, which is why Agent Derringer was here."

"Agent Derringer?" Bella echoed. "Is that the man who just left?"

Richard looked at Jax, who bowed his head to study his clasped hands. The senior constable cleared his throat. "Yes, he was leaving when you came in, Arabella. He's a federal prohibition agent. A senior one. The cousins are involved with bootlegging, along with disposing of Miss Crabtree's body and automobile, and getting rid of Mrs. Ryerson's car." He paused for a moment. "There's still a search going on for Miss Crabtree and the vehicles. Along the lake."

Richard's revelations presented a tragic image, but Bella wondered about the agent. "Mr. Anderson mentioned his relatives making runs from Canada. They must be part of a bigger operation if a federal agent is taking an interest."

"Evidently, they are," Richard said. "Bringing booze across the lake is becoming more and more common. From Ohio, it's taken to various states for distribution. This is early in the season for shipments, which is why Lansing and Anderson could have gotten into Canada easily. In another couple of weeks, Derringer will have men on the lookout for bootleggers."

"Were Miss Lansing and Mr. Anderson involved in rumrunning?" Bella asked.

"Mr. Anderson, maybe. He didn't answer our questions," Nolen replied. "We don't think Miss Lansing was. She was mainly interested in Miss Crabtree's money."

Because Jax had so little to say, Bella glanced at him. His head was bowed, which increased her dread. As she had many times in the past fifteen months, she felt a gap widening between them. She desperately wanted to hurry this meeting along and talk with him before the gap became a chasm.

"Derringer is headed to interrogate Anderson and his relatives, so he'll know more later today, or so we hope." Richard leaned back in his chair. "He and Lansing will face several serious charges: two counts of kidnapping and one murder, not to mention robbery. Anderson probably can't lessen his sentence by cooperating, but his cousins might do themselves some good by revealing their bootlegging partners."

"Their cooperation should help Agent Derringer catch a lot of rumrunners," Nolen said.

"He needs help," Richard observed. "He's got a hard job and not nearly enough men or money to do it." He glanced at Jax. "No wonder he's always trying to recruit more good men."

The comment, and Jax's failure to respond, sent fresh anxiety through Bella, but she didn't voice her concerns. They needed to wrap up the case. When everyone else left, she'd get answers from Jax.

Chapter Fourteen

T HIRTY MINUTES LATER, THEY finished the wrap up. Richard got to his feet, shook hands with Nolen and Jax, and nodded to Bella. "I want to get on the road for home." He looked at Jax. "I know you plan to leave within the week, but an exact day will help Jenny and me plan. In the meantime, take care of that fresh wound."

"I should make the rounds now," Nolen said before rushing after the senior constable.

Although Bella wanted to talk with Jax about his revelations concerning her brother's death, she wondered why Richard was coming back and where Jax was going. The senior constable's remark about Derringer looking for good men weighed too heavily on her mind not to start there. "Where are you going next week? Is that when Lansing and Anderson will be tried? I didn't think the court date would be set so soon." Even as she asked the questions, Bella felt her uneasiness grow. He finally looked at her, but his blank expression was impossible to read.

"No court date is set for Lansing and Anderson. I'll be back when one is, if it doesn't come up before I leave, which is unlikely."

Her heart hammered hard against her ribs. His words, expression, and tone all combined to increase her sense of foreboding. "Where are you going?" she asked again.

Jax's nostrils flared with a sharp intake of breath, but he held her gaze. "Derringer asked me a while back to join his team. I wasn't sure about it then..."

When his voice trailed off, Bella didn't need to be told where Jax was going or what he was doing. Nolen and Richard had revealed enough information for her to guess. She figured she knew why, too. "You're sure now, though." An icy knot of dread gripped her heart as she waited for confirmation of her fears.

He nodded. "Yes, I am. That's why Richard is coming back. He'll be the acting constable. With two deputies and a part-time clerk, he can handle things for the foreseeable future."

"You're leaving Moreley." She was stating the obvious, but clear thinking again proved problematic. When he'd rushed away from her yesterday afternoon, Bella hadn't figured he'd go so far or so fast. She hadn't been as confident as Ida about a fortunate outcome, but she hadn't figured he'd take off, either.

"I am."

Hot tears pricked the backs of her eyes, and Bella blinked quickly to keep them from spilling down her face. "You're doing this because you feel guilty about Matt, and you shouldn't."

Jax braced his elbows on the table and put his head in his hands. "Don't make this any harder than it is."

His admission and posture sent a sliver of light into the darkness shrouding her. If going was hard for him, that was a positive sign. "I plan to make it as difficult as possible."

When he lifted his head, Jax looked confused. "Why? Surely, you're glad you can come to town and not see me."

Her heart twisted. Jax appeared stricken. "No, I'm not glad at all. I'll be sad," she admitted. As she spoke, her confidence grew. Once Jax knew her true sentiments, he shouldn't be so troubled. "You ran off yesterday without giving me a chance to absorb your revelations. Now, you're running even farther, and you don't need to do that for me. I don't blame you for Matt dying. Not at all."

His jaw tightened until a muscle jumped spasmodically. "Someone else could have gone in my place. It didn't need to be Matt, and it wouldn't have been if I'd kept my mouth shut and agreed with him about another officer going."

"He might have offered that idea before thinking it over. But my brother wouldn't have wanted just anyone in your place, not when some of your men were our friends and neighbors. He cared about them, too. No matter what you said, in the end, he would have gone, Jax. You know he would have." Jax stared at her for a seemingly limitless time, but said nothing. Just as he turned his head, Bella saw his eyes become damp with moisture. Before he could hide his expression, she lightly clasped his jaw. "You know I'm right."

His golden lashes fluttered down. "If I'd gone back to the line, Matt would be here now."

"You can't be sure of that. The war lasted another seven weeks. He might not have gotten home anyhow."

Jax opened his eyes and gazed back at her. "Bella, your brother died in my place. That's all that really matters."

When he would have glanced away, she tightened her grasp on his jaw. "What happened that first time you were wounded? Was it when your bicep was damaged?"

Shock blanketed his face. "Who told you about my bicep?"

If she'd had any lingering doubt, the question would been the final indication that Jax had taken the blame for something not his fault. "Doc Smedlay mentioned it yesterday." When he closed his eyes again, she realized he was still hiding the complete truth from her, most likely because he'd never been honest with himself. "Why didn't you tell me about it?" She released her hold on him but maintained a steady gaze.

He ran one hand over his face in a gesture of fatigue and frustration, but he finally looked back at her. "The damage makes playing golf difficult, but it wouldn't have kept me from being with my men."

Slowly but surely, more information arose from the recesses of her mind. "You're right-handed. How would you have used your sidearm with a wound to your bicep?"

"It wouldn't have been that difficult," he replied.

Exasperation filled her. "What did the doctors say?"

His gaze skittered away, and he said nothing.

A long sigh left Bella. "Your failure to answer my questions is proof you weren't being sent back by the doctors. The fact that your commanding officer approved the change is proof he knew you weren't ready and, if Matt offered to take your place, he saw that, as well. Saw it and didn't want just anyone with your men." She stopped for a heartbeat. "Who decided you should go back to the line, Jax? The doctors or you?"

When he looked back at her, anguish darkened his gaze. Moments passed before Jax spoke. "All right. The doctors wanted me to stay a little longer, but I was good enough to go back. I know I was, and I know I should have gone. Or I should have let someone else go. Not Matt."

His tone was as flat and hard and dark as a blackboard, while his words scratched across it like fingernails. The combination made her cringe. How could she get through to him when he kept repeating the same things? Clearly, his words and feelings had been in his mind for two-and-a-half years. Letting go of those beliefs was understandably difficult. But she wanted to make sure he did. Even if Jax left Moreley for good, he shouldn't haul guilt with him.

"Stop blaming yourself for Matt's death. I don't. He wouldn't." Bella clasped his arm. Beneath her fingers, the muscles tensed. "I've gone over and over what you said. I've thought about everything, and you would have done the same for Matt, if the situation had been reversed."

"You don't know that," he said in a choked whisper.

"Yes, I do because I know you. You aren't a coward. I'm so sorry you've been blaming yourself all this time, although I can't say I'm surprised." Bits and pieces of the past had already returned to her, and they resurfaced now. Jax was overly conscientious and always had been. She wouldn't lose sight of that again.

Confusion clouded his gaze when he looked back at her. "What do you mean?"

"You've always taken responsibility for things that weren't your fault. Remember when Sadie Connors and I were smoking cigarettes behind the golf shop? We were foolish enough to leave the butts behind. You cleaned them up. When my father saw you, he said you were aware of the rules about caddies smoking on the grounds. He suspended you for a week. No caddying, no golf. But you still took the blame for us."

"That was nothing."

"Nothing? Your father added to the penalty by not allowing you at Ballantyne for a month. A month at the start of the golf season, and he assigned you to digging ditches in your free time. I saw the blisters covering your hands. You couldn't hold a golf club at the end of the four weeks."

"It wasn't a big deal, Bella." His tone was emotionless.

She shook her head. "It was a big deal to me. I should have spoken up, but I knew my parents wouldn't let me play in the Invertone Ladies Amateur if I'd told the truth. I've always felt bad about it, and I should have apologized long before now."

He looked back at her then. "You don't owe me an apology. It was your first trip to that tournament. I didn't want it spoiled for you."

"The point is, you took the blame for me."

"That's one distant instance," he pointed out. "It doesn't establish a pattern."

His stubborn resistance annoyed her, but she pressed on. "Then, there was the time Rodney Fleming took tools from the hardware. You were there and tried to stop him, but he ran off. Mr. Habestall told your dad that two kids had been around when the items came up missing, so your father spoke to you first. Because Rodney's dad would have thrashed him, you took the blame for that, too."

Surprise blanketed his face. "Who told you about that?"

"Matt."

Jax's expression softened. "I shouldn't be surprised."

"Probably not, and it proves my point."

"Which is?"

She pursed her lips before replying. Such obstinacy. He couldn't be more hard-headed if he'd had a helmet permanently attached to his skull. "You take the blame for things that aren't your fault. You always have. I suppose you always will, but you can't continue to condemn yourself for Matt's death. He wouldn't blame you, and you know it." When he said nothing, she continued. "You know I'm right, Jax." Would he finally agree?

As her statement hung in the air between them, Jax shifted restlessly. Why did she have to make assertions that couldn't honestly be refuted? Matt wouldn't have blamed him, and Jax would have given his life for his friend without a second's hesitation, but his guilt over Matt's death had become part of him. It was so ingrained that letting it go seemed like losing some of himself. "I don't know..." he said in an indistinct murmur.

"You've obviously blamed yourself for a long time, but it's a burden you need to put down. I miss Matt terribly, but I've missed you, too. You've kept everyone at a distance since the war." She offered a tremulous smile. "Now, I can see that your self-imposed guilt over Matt's death is the reason."

Jax weighed her words. They didn't completely penetrate the cloud of remorse surrounding him, but they shone light into it. Because he saw his regret and shame weren't only hurting him, they were hurting people around him, Jax was honest when he replied. "Yes, I've been torn up with guilt, and I couldn't talk about it. I couldn't talk about Matt. It's still hard. I keep wishing it was possible to go back in time and return to the line while he went on leave."

Bella bit her lower lip. "I can understand that, but your coldness hurt."

His heart thundered in his chest. Everything in him wanted to reach out to her, to shoulder some of her grief, to offer the comfort he should have provided in France. But he was going away in a few days and didn't know when he'd be back. "I appreciate your willingness to forgive me, just like I appreciate you and Mac welcoming me at Ballantyne. It was always a second home to me."

"It still can be," she murmured.

The assertion shattered the last of his reserve. "Thank you. I'm grateful." Unsure what else to say, Jax hesitated.

"You missed Easter, but I hope you'll come more often and not only for holidays."

While the warmth in her words and expression were compelling, the statement served as a reminder that he wouldn't be able to drop in at Ballantyne. Not for a while, at least. "I can't do that in the immediate future." When her good humor evaporated, he inwardly cursed himself. Why had he accepted Derringer's offer so quickly? But could he have turned it down? Not in all good conscience.

She wrapped her arms around her middle as if warding off a stomach ache. "You're still leaving."

Her bleak expression added to Jax's discontent and made him want to say something to ease the new breach between them. She didn't blame him for her brother's death, which was far more than he could have expected. That should have eased their situation, and it probably would have if he hadn't accepted Derringer's offer. Once again, he thought about Miss Crabtree and Grover Hilliard. They'd wasted years because of her pride. Now, it was too late for them. Not wanting to make the same mistake, Jax provided more explanation. "Derringer presented a convincing case this morning. One I can't turn my back on."

"Why did he persuade you today?"

Jax slumped back in the chair and met her gaze. "He told me about a fellow army officer, Mick O'Donnelly, someone I knew in the war. His wife was murdered by a hitman."

Bella's jaw dropped. "Why?"

"Mick is a prohibition agent. He'd worked a big case back east, put some bootleggers in jail, and was going after more of them." Jax folded his arms across his chest. "Last Sunday, he and his family were walking home from church. His wife, their five-year-old boy, and their infant girl, who was in a baby carriage, were with him. Mick walked ahead to open their front gate. An automobile sped by and gunfire erupted." His voice became ragged, and Jax cleared his throat. "His wife was hit four times. She died on the sidewalk in front of him and their children."

Bella's hand flew to her mouth. "How horrible."

"It doesn't get much worse. Of course, Derringer and others in the Prohibition Bureau are making this case a top priority. Mick O'Donnelly is a good man, and he's completely shattered."

"I'm sure he is, but you're taking a very dangerous job."

"It is, but it's something I have to do." Jax wanted her to understand, so he continued. "Mick was one of the guys who helped Nolen get me off the battlefield when I was wounded the first time. He was already married, and they had one child. Even so, he didn't think twice about risking his life for me. Now, I need to repay him by seeing his wife's killer is caught."

Several moments of silence ticked away. Bella folded her hands on the table and stared down at them. "Good luck. I hope all goes well."

Her tone and posture grated on Jax. This was not the response he'd expected. "It's the right thing for me to do, Bella. Surely, you can see that."

Almost immediately, her head jerked up. "You always do the right thing, Jax, or what you think is the right thing. You didn't reveal Alan's betrayal of Ida because it was right to keep a promise. You didn't tell me why you felt guilty about Matt's death because that seemed right, and you offered to be a substitute big brother, because that was right, too. You tried to keep me out of all four of your big cases here because that appeared to be right." Her nostrils flared with a sharp intake of breath and her chin lifted a fraction. "It's funny how the right thing always keeps us apart. But maybe we should be." A weak laugh left her. "Of course, since you're leaving, we will be."

The assertions slashed through Jax, and when Bella stood, he did, too. As she turned away, he grasped her arm. "Don't leave like this." Should he say he'd be back? Would he? Bella was right about the danger in his new job. Despite those facts, Jax didn't want a clean break. Or a break at all. He wanted another chance, but would he live long enough to get one? He wasn't sure, and trying to establish some tie now—when he was leaving for an indeterminate time to go into a perilous situation—would be selfish. Not that Bella wanted ties now. Her lovely features looked like a frozen mask. He'd never seen her appear so distant and icy. Ever since marching off to war, he'd regretted not revealing his feelings. Did he want to die with the same remorse?

No, he didn't. His heart raced as he leaned forward. With one hand, he cupped her cheek. Briefly, surprise flashed in her gaze, but she didn't move away. "There's something I've been wanting to do for a long, long time."

Her dark eyes warmed, but for several moments, she said nothing. The color in her face deepened as Bella grasped his wrist. "It might be the same thing I've wanted to do for a long, long time." Her voice was a hushed murmur.

Jax lowered his head and let his lips lightly brush hers. She laid her hands on his shoulders and rose to press her mouth against his. While the kiss went on, he let his fingers caress her silky hair. The short bob looked pretty, but felt even better. Abruptly, the telephone in the outer office rang. He froze. Why a call now?

After another ring, Bella pulled her hands away from him. "Shouldn't you get that?"

Her breath fanned his mouth, so forming a reply was difficult. "I suppose so. After all, I'm still the constable here until the end of next week." He released her and stepped back.

"Will you be home at all while you're working the case?"

Chances of getting home were virtually nil. Derringer had made that clear. No time off. "Probably not." When she squared her shoulders, Jax figured Bella was gathering her defenses. Part of him still wanted to ask for some tenuous commitment, but was that wise? If he got back in one piece, Jax would pursue a courtship. Nothing would stand in his way unless Bella didn't share his feelings. But her kiss gave him hope. When the telephone began jangling again, Jax swore under his breath. "I better answer." When he did, Jax felt worse than ever. He turned to Bella, who had followed him to the counter. "It's for you. Biggins."

Jax didn't step away as Bella spoke to the golf pro. Instead, he listened to every word, and his spirits sank lower and lower. When she hung up, her words didn't surprise him.

"I need to get back to Ballantyne."

"Of course." For a moment, she gazed at him, but he was unable to gauge her thoughts.

"Keep in touch, if you can and take care of yourself."

"You do the same," he replied. When she turned away, he hurried on, "And don't get involved in any investigations while I'm gone." Bella paused, but didn't look back.

"Let's hope I don't need to."

Before he could offer another admonition, she was gone. Her parting salvo put him on edge, and so did Biggins' call. The man had said he and Bella had an *engagement*. Did they really? Jax touched his lips, still tingling from her kiss. He knew Bella well, had known her for almost all of his life. She wouldn't kiss him and step out with another man.

Jax planned to be careful in the new job, and he'd make sure he got back to Moreley in one piece. He tried not to think about what might happen in his absence.

Bella headed toward the Model T but, when she reached it, she didn't get in. Jax admitted wanting to kiss her for a long time, and she'd revealed the same wish. As she thought about the light brush of his lips on hers, warmth spread through Bella. Would they have kissed again if Griff hadn't telephoned? Probably so. Bella was sorry she'd promised to play golf with their new pro and Ida. If she hadn't, no call would have interrupted. Annoyance, mostly at herself, filled her. If not for that call, she and Jax would still be kissing.

Anxiety followed. When would Jax be back? Would he be back? He'd survived the war, and now he was putting his life on the line again. She understood wanting justice for his friend, who was grief-stricken. Jax's loyalty, sense of responsibility, and self-sacrifice were admirable traits. But they were also impediments to making a commitment.

She'd told him as much, and his answer had been a kiss.

Interesting, but it didn't mean he wanted a commitment. Did he? Perhaps not. Why hadn't he asked her to wait? Why hadn't he said he'd try to get back? Because he didn't want to do either? Or because the possibility was nil? The latter seemed more like Jax. He'd see the investigation through, to help his friend.

Being a prohibition agent wasn't as hazardous as serving as a line officer during the war. But it wasn't safe, either. Far from it.

The thoughts rambled around in her head. No real resolution resulted. She swiveled toward the constable's office. When she'd said her final goodbye, Jax had looked stricken. Why? She could have said more. She should have said more. That certainty had her crossing the road and going back into the building.

As the doorbell jingled, he called out. "In my office."

Bella didn't reply. Instead, she hurried toward the sound of his voice. Surprise blanketed his face when he saw her. "Bella. Is something wrong?" He rose to his feet but didn't move toward her.

"Only one thing." She crossed the room and went to stand beside him.

"What?"

A knot of emotion clogged her throat, which made speaking difficult. Once again, Bella reminded herself that she was a modern woman. Not a flapper, but not a shy girl, either. She laid one hand on his cheek. "You said you waited a long, long time to kiss me. How long?"

Briefly, his eyes closed. When they opened, they glittered with warmth and more. "Years and years."

She couldn't repress a grin. "Two years?" He shook his head. "Four years?" He shook it again. Bella's eyes widened. "Six years?"

This time, he spoke his reply. "Since you were fifteen, and I was seventeen."

Astonishment held her momentarily mute. She hadn't anticipated that answer. Kissing back then would have been highly inappropriate. Not that she hadn't thought about it herself.

"Not as long for you," he said with a trace of disappointment in his deep voice.

"Exactly as long," she admitted.

He beamed at her. "I never guessed."

"Never?" As a youngster, she'd feared her crush was obvious to everyone.

"Not back then. Maybe later." A shrug lifted his freshly wounded arm, which made him wince.

Her good humor left. "You should be at home resting, not working."

"I'm all right." His gaze scanned her face. "Why did you come back, Bella? Don't you have an engagement with Biggins? He said you did."

A frown furrowed her brow. "We're supposed to play golf with Ida is all," she replied. "And I came back because..."

"Because why?"

She sighed. "Because I didn't want to leave without knowing if you'll try to get home while you're with the bureau. If you'll want to get home." Her confidence was lagging. "This doesn't sound proper. I like to think I'm a modern young woman, but I was raised with the rule that girls don't chase after boys. All of us were. Most females still are."

Jax rolled his eyes. "You chased after your brother and me all the time. You wanted to do everything we did. Your father, grandfather, and Mac had the devil of a time keeping you from trying to caddy. Not that any men and few women would have hired you. They'd have been scandalized." A laugh left him. "You hated skirts and wore Matt's cast-off knickers every chance you got until you were fifteen and your mother stopped you. Not to mention that..."

Bella held up a hand. "Enough. You made your point." Heat climbed into her cheeks. "What I'm talking about is different."

His expression softened. "Coming back now isn't chasing after me. Neither is asking if I'll be home occasionally. And I wouldn't be scandalized, if you did." When she moved her hand, still on his cheek, Jax gently clasp it. "Derringer said not to expect much time off."

As Bella stepped away, Jax put his free hand on her waist and brought her closer. "I'll be in Philadelphia. If I can make it home for even a day, I will. I probably won't know ahead, though." His thumb gently stroked her cheek. "I can't make other promises now. It wouldn't be right." Abruptly, he stopped. A troubled frown knit his brow. "I know you didn't want to hear that."

"No, not really," she admitted, "but you wouldn't be you without wanting to do the right thing."

He nodded. "I'll try to get back here when I can, if I can. And I'll write, if you'd like that."

"I would. Can I write to you, too?"

"When I have an address, I'll send it along. Until then, this will have to do." He bent his head and pressed his lips to hers.

Bella wrapped her arms around his neck and felt his arms go around her. Oddly, time passed both quickly and slowly but, at some point, the front doorbell jingled and they reluctantly broke apart. When she looked at Jax again, Bella couldn't repress a smile.

"Jax?" A voice called from the front.

"Just a minute," he replied.

After one last featherlight kiss, Jax moved away from Bella. She reluctantly released her hold on him. "I better go." A lingering goodbye wouldn't help.

"Take care of yourself, Bella."

"You do the same." Because Bella didn't want another long-lasting impasse, she went on. "And come back safe and sound and soon."

A smile lit his handsome face. "That's my plan."

Moments later, Bella was on the road to Ballantyne. Her heart was full, mostly with joy and hope, but a trace of doubt crept in. Both she and Jax had plans before the war, and plans too often had to be changed. She forced that knowledge to a far corner of her mind. Time would tell what the future held—for better or for worse.

About the Author

D.S. Lang write historical mysteries set in America after the Great War. They feature intrepid women sleuths focused on cracking cases. She started making up stories to entertain herself as an only child, and she is still making them up. Now, she puts them in writing.

After earning Bachelor's and Master's degrees in education, D.S. worked as a golf shop manager, teacher (junior high, high school, and college), program manager, tutor, and mentor. She has a life-long love of history and often gets sidetracked on research when she should be writing.

When she is away from the computer, D.S. enjoys reading, swimming, spending time with family and friends, and walking her dog Izzy

Afterword

Thank you for reading <u>A Baffling Absence</u>! If you have time, please review or rate the book. That helps other readers find new authors and new books. You can sign up for my newsletter at my website. You will also find me on Goodreads and BookBub.

Books in the Arabella Stewart Historical Mystery Series

For more information on her other books, historical tidbits, book club questions, and more, please visit https://www.dslangbooks.com

www.ingramcontent.com/pod-product-compliance
Lightning Source LLC
Chambersburg PA
CBHW051337020726
47501CB00007B/2130